A WOLF OF HIS OWN

By Fleur Blüm

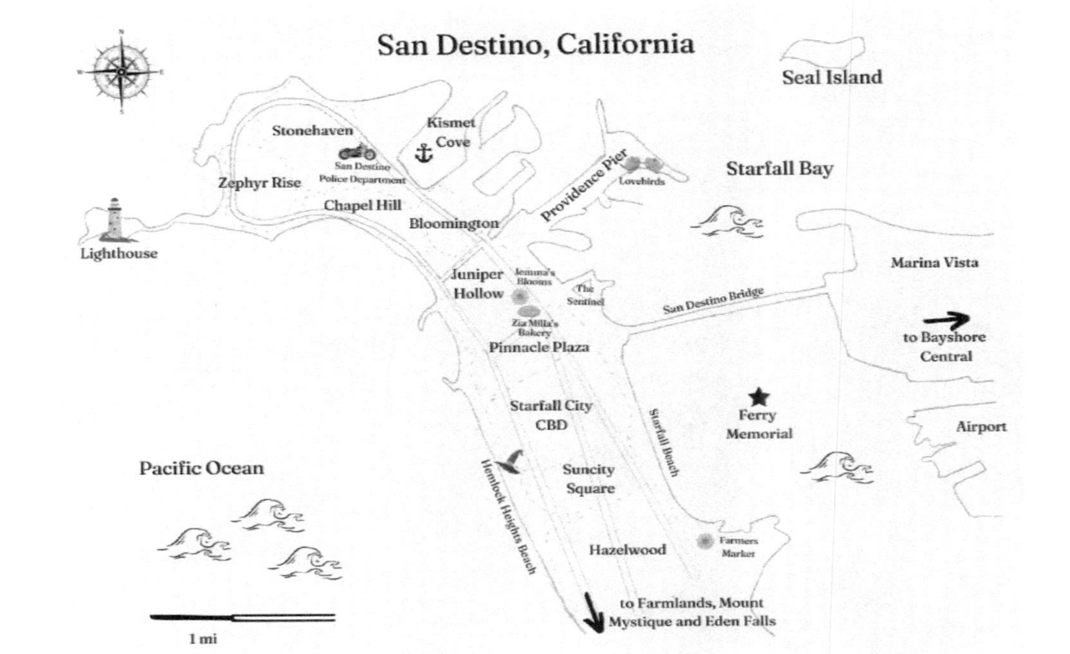

San Destino, California
Seal Island
Stonehaven
Kismet Cove
Zephyr Rise
San Destino Police Department
Providence Pier
Lovebirds
Starfall Bay
Chapel Hill
Bloomington
Lighthouse
Juniper Hollow
Jemma's Blooms
The Sentinel
San Destino Bridge
Marina Vista
Zia Milla's Bakery
Pinnacle Plaza
to Bayshore Central
Starfall City CBD
Ferry Memorial
Airport
Starfall Beach
Pacific Ocean
Suncity Square
Hemlock Heights Beach
Hazelwood
Farmers Market
to Farmlands, Mount Mystique and Eden Falls
1 mi

Fleur Blüm is a Melbourne-based writer, performer and musician.

Her blog can be found at https://fleurblum.com/blog

Also by Fleur Blüm
Sophie's Path: A choose your own romance adventure
Discovering the Franklins
My Mother's Secret
The Sins of the Father: a Barrett Women novel
The Mother's Fault: a Barrett Women novel
Singular Focus
Singular Purpose
Morgana, My Queen
Pillion for a Police Officer
Carter & Carter Detective Agency

Poetry Collections:
My Body. No Apology
Consider the Watchmaker
Smells Like Teen Angst

The characters and incidents portrayed herein are fictitious. Any similarity to a name, character, or history of any actual person, living or dead, is entirely coincidental.

First edition 2025

Copyright © 2025 Fleur Blüm
ISBN: 978-1-7641261-0-6

Editor: Sarah Lamb
Cover Design: Get Covers

Published by Fleur Blüm, Melbourne, Australia

Chapter 1

Officer Jason Bell adjusted the belt on his hips. He still wasn't used to carrying so much; handcuffs, sidearm, radio, flashlight, pepper spray, and baton. The first day he'd put it on, he'd felt like Batman with his utility belt, exciting and powerful, but now it felt heavy and he was sweating beneath the poly-wool blend of his uniform. He was still in long sleeves too, not yet having been given permission to wear short sleeves. All of which would have been fine if it weren't the hottest Fourth of July they'd had for years.

He'd been paired up with Sergeant Riley Holmes again, which he was pleased about. Riley was not a big woman, with short dark hair, but she exuded authority. She also wasn't technically a training officer, or TO, and so he only got paired with her when they were short staffed, but she saw him as a human being, and not some sort of tool to be used as she saw fit like some of the others.

"Stop fidgeting, Bell. I know you're hot, so am I, but we're here to ensure public order and fidgeting doesn't inspire confidence or order."

"Yes, ma'am."

A frown flickered across Holmes' face, as though she was considering telling—again—that he didn't need to call her ma'am, but she said nothing. Her eyes slid back to the festivities in Juniper Hollow, scanning the crowd for suspicious activity.

The other reason he liked Riley was she was queer. Despite not having mentioned his sexuality to anyone at the station, they all behaved as though he had. His small stature and angular, elfin features didn't help either. Riley wasn't officially out at work, and hadn't told him in so many words, but he'd seen her out with her girlfriend, a stunning redhead called Petra.

"You got plans for later?" Riley asked.

"Nah, I'm not much for big celebrations. Plus, all this standing out in the sun has taken it out of me." He glanced at his watch, only a couple of hours till knockoff, then he'd trudge home to Hazelwood for a cold shower and an early night.

Riley turned to him, her mouth hitched in a half-smile. "You are a bit of a homebody, aren't you?"

He shrugged.

"I might head to Jack's Bar after work. Ward invited everyone who's been on crowd duty. We might even get a free beer out of it."

Watch Commander Ward wasn't one to be generous in Jason's experience.

"I guess I could be convinced. Ask me again at the end of the shift." He stood up a little straighter and tried to reframe his thoughts to include a couple of cold ones later. He wasn't rostered tomorrow, and it might make him seem more like one of the boys to go.

*

Roman Eldritch stretched his neck, rolling it from one shoulder to the other, as he took a brief break from the hustle and bustle behind the bar at Jack's. He'd accepted a double shift today, with Independence Day celebrations set to pack all the venues in San Destino, especially those on Providence Pier, like Jack's. The sound system was cranking garish pop songs and new electronic tracks, neither of which was Roman's style. He preferred the more elegant sounds of 40s and 50s jazz, but whenever he mentioned it to Patrice, the owner, she looked at him with her dead-eyed stare and he dropped the subject.

It was probably fair enough, the crowd here weren't interested in his anachronistic musical taste, but it did make those nights when the band were able to play all the more special.

"Roman? Get your butt back out here, will you?" Patrice called, her booming voice carrying over the thumping music into the storeroom where he had been hiding out. He straightened up, tucked the tails of his black button-down shirt back into his black dress pants where they'd come loose, grabbed the bottle of bourbon he'd come in for, and walked out into the mêlée once more.

"What can I get you?" he said, leaning over the polished wood bar to the next customer, a gorgeous young man, his short blond hair looking tousled, but not in a cool way—more like he'd been working hard. His angular face was accentuated by the smooth skin of his jaw. The patch between his eyebrows crinkled in concern, making him look a little like a deer in headlights.

"Can I get two draft beers? I guess something light."

Roman narrowed his eyes, he looked very young. "Can I see your ID?"

"Sure," the young man reached back for his wallet and showed his ID, which indicated he was twenty-two. His name was Jason Bell, not that Roman should have been looking at that, but the name tickled something in the back of his mind.

"You sure that's not a fake?" Roman asked, his lips curling into a grin at the startled look on the young man's face.

"No, uh…" he stammered and looked over to the group of off-duty cops who were monopolizing one of the booths.

"You're with those guys? You seem young to be a cop." This was too easy. Roman knew he shouldn't tease the poor guy, but his face was so expressive.

"I'm still a rookie, but yeah, you can ask my colleagues if you think my ID is fake."

"Don't stress, Sunshine, I believe you. Two draft beers coming up." He put his best friendly smile on and hoped the wolfish glee inside didn't show through. He pulled two pale ales from the pumps a little way along the bar and brought them back to Jason.

"Here we are," he said, plonking the two glasses on the bar and putting his hand out to take Jason's cash. A large, ruddy-faced, ginger-haired man squeezed himself beside Jason and started clicking his fingers at Roman.

Who taught this buffoon manners? Jason's eyes widened a little at the man before he took a half-step back to allow him room.

"I'll be with you in just a moment, sir." Roman turned to get Jason's change and did his best to hide the annoyance towards this brutish, entitled man. When he returned, Jason took his change, nodded, and headed back towards the other off duty cops, but as he was behind the buffoon he rolled his eyes—it was a fleeting movement, but it made Roman smile. He always disliked people who thought they were better than servers.

"What can I get you?" he asked the burly gentleman.

"I'm buying a round for the crew; I'll have twelve of whatever Tinkerbell just bought."

It took everything in Roman's power to keep his anger and disgust from showing on his face. Tinkerbell? What a nasty nickname for such an attractive young man. He hoped it was just a dig about his size and features, and not homophobic as well, though it wouldn't surprise him either way. Cops had a reputation for treating minorities with utter disrespect.

"Coming right up. I can bring them over if you like."

The large man nodded and paid with his card. Roman turned away to pull the beers for this oaf, allowing the action to distract and calm him. It was unusual for him to be so incensed on behalf of someone he'd barely exchanged words with, but there was something in those delicate features that brought out the protective streak in him.

*

Jason could have sworn he'd just shared something with the bartender; a mutual dislike of Ward's attitude to service staff yes, but perhaps something more. He was never sure when someone was flirting with him. There was always a risk of misreading friendliness as attraction and, given his work colleagues weren't officially aware of his sexuality, it seemed like the worst possible time to think about pursuing something.

The other cops from the shift were sitting like they owned the place, taking over a booth and dragging over chairs from nearby tables. They were boisterous and all several beers in by this stage. Jason had never felt comfortable at these gatherings, and would much rather have been at home, in a nice cool bath or with a chilled rosé, but whenever he refused his colleagues made such a fuss, he decided it was some sort of mandatory bonding.

Apart from Riley, there were only a handful of female officers in the San Destino Police Department. The new Chief of Police, Brody Hale, was doing what he could to make the culture more welcoming, and Jason had seen posters around town trying to interest women in joining the force, but it hadn't made much of a dent so far. Being small of frame, and closeted, Jason felt out of place in the male-dominated workplace, though on the job, it was usually just him and his training officer, which was more tolerable. In these social settings, the number of hyper-masculine men around him rose, as did his stress levels. It was one thing to be teased for being a bit camp, and not having a girlfriend, but if his colleagues knew he was gay, he expected the bullying to escalate.

And yet, his thoughts went back to the man behind the bar, a few inches taller than Jason, with broad shoulders, dark brown hair, and almost golden hazel eyes. His stubble was trimmed neatly, and his black button-down shirt was open low enough to show off his impressive chest hair. Jason wondered what he smelled like; it should be woody, perhaps smoky—like a lumberjack, though he would probably smell like beer, and whatever cologne he was wearing.

"You doing anything on your days off, Bell?" Riley had appeared at his side. She seemed to have taken him under her wing since they'd spent a few shifts together.

"Not really. Mom wants me to pop in and say hello. They have an Independence Day party every year, but obviously I couldn't go today."

"You could still go. I'm sure this lot would forgive leaving to take care of family business. You've made an appearance."

Jason shifted on his seat. "Because saying I'm leaving to see my mother is going to do great things for my reputation. Plus, I don't really like her parties—too many women trying to organize my life, no room to breathe."

Riley chuckled. "I wouldn't know what that's like, but I get your point... You let me know if the hazing gets out of line, won't you? A bit of ribbing is one thing, but out and out harassment is another."

"I shouldn't have said anything. It's fine, really. What about you? Are you and Petra doing anything?"

"She's waiting for me at my place," Riley said, rubbing her hand through her short, dark hair. The silly grin she got on her face any time Petra was mentioned was glorious to behold; she didn't smile much. Jason's mind wandered back to that lovely bartender, and whether one day he might find someone who made him glow like that with his own private happiness. "I have the late shift tomorrow, so we'll have a sleep in and maybe grab lunch somewhere."

"It sounds very domestic."

"It is. I'm very lucky to have found someone who knows me like she does."

One of the other officers turned to them and started asking Riley about a case they'd worked on together. Jason was thankful for the volume of chatter and music in the bar, knowing that while Riley didn't hide her sexuality or her relationship, no one else in the station knew about Petra. Jason leaned back, taking a sip of his beer, savoring the cool, smooth texture in his mouth after a long, hot day.

I wonder when I can safely leave without getting shit about it. Jason looked around his companions and decided it would be at least another beer each before they were distracted enough that he could slip away.

"I think you left this at the bar," a smooth smoky voice purred in his ear. Jason jumped and turned towards the voice to find the distracting bartender hovering next to his shoulder. He held out a folded white napkin.

"I… uh, don't think so." Jason's throat started to heat.

"You definitely did; look at it later." The bartender pushed the napkin into the pocket of Jason's shirt. He smelled different, and yet exactly as Jason had imagined; leather, rosemary, and something he couldn't quite pinpoint. The heat radiating from his body was not helping with the flush Jason was sure was traveling up his neck and face.

"Thank you," was all Jason managed to say before the bartender turned and walked away. He'd been so close, and none of his colleagues had picked up on what Jason would have sworn was a giant neon flashing sign over his head announcing the interaction.

Riley looked at him sideways, a small smile on her lips, before she returned her attention to the guy talking to her.

At least I didn't imagine it. He wanted desperately to look at the napkin, but he would wait until he was outside, away from the curious eyes of his coworkers. They might have missed the bartender's visit, but they would want to know what the note said if he pulled it out now.

One of the slowest hours of Jason's life unfolded after the bartender slipped him the napkin, before he decided to leave. Riley had excused herself about ten minutes before, but she was a sergeant, a great cop by all accounts despite having stayed in patrol, and as a rookie, he was under heavier scrutiny.

Jason slipped away without saying goodbye; the group was drunk enough that he could say he had, and they wouldn't be likely to remember differently. He tried to catch the bartender's eye as he walked by, but he was serving drinks, the bar was now three people deep as though they had all decided to get top-ups just as he was leaving.

The air outside had cooled a little, though it was still uncomfortably hot. Fourth of July revelers were still out. The pier was heavy with them, some canoodling, some having loud conversations perhaps fighting or perhaps not, it was hard to tell. He was glad to have been on the day shift today, making sure people didn't disrupt the parade, and not on the late shift, trying to keep order among the intoxicated chaos and inevitable illegal fireworks.

The summer had been hot very early this year, and the solstice festivities had been even bigger than this—he'd been on shift that night, and had seen some strange goings on, not least of which was a group of young women running through Juniper Hollow stark naked.

Jason's house was about fifteen minutes' walk from the pier. He liked to use the time to decompress from the day, and make sure he wasn't bringing any of the energy of his shift back to his roommates. There were things he saw as a cop that made him shudder. The careless cruelty of human beings was something he didn't think he'd ever get over, though it was a small city and he had mostly had to deal with drunkenness and petty theft so far.

As he made his way over Bridge Road, with Destiny Bridge to his left, the wind changed and blew a chill across the water. Jason shivered and put his hands into the pockets of his chinos. After another minute or so, it started to rain. Only lightly at first, but soon it was coming down in fat, summer-rainstorm drops. He wasn't far from home, and he decided to jog the last few hundred yards in an effort to stay dry.

By the time he was at his front door, his shirt was soaked through, and water ran off his hair into his eyes.

So much for staying dry. He put his key in the lock and opened the door trying to keep the squeak to a minimum, but he failed at that too. As he toed off his shoes in the front hallway, he remembered the napkin in his front pocket. Carefully, he pulled the pocket open, and extracted the flimsy, wet paper.

There were smudges of black and purple where the ink had run. Jason unfolded it, doing his best not to tear it, only to find the big smudges that might have been a name and phone number were completely illegible.

"Shit," he muttered to himself. He took the napkin to his room, where he laid it on his desk, hoping the numbers would be easier to read when it had dried out. He stripped off his wet clothes, wrung them out in the bathroom sink, and had a shower before crawling into bed, dreaming of a rosemary scented man whose name he didn't know.

Chapter 2

The Independence Day celebrations had meant the bar was even busier than a normal Friday night, and Roman didn't get home until nearly daybreak. He showered and crawled into bed, knowing he was back at the bar that night for his other job, playing saxophone in the house jazz band.

For a while, Roman had thought he might be able to make a living from his music. He'd studied at the Conservatory of Music just over the bridge on the mainland and had been one of their rising stars. But then he finished college and had to face the reality of a musician's life. He sometimes got gigs playing at weddings or other big events, and a few times a year he would be invited to play with a bigger orchestra on the mainland, but it wasn't enough to live on.

He'd worked at Jack's all through college, and when he graduated, he stayed on. They would roster him on as Assistant Manager some shifts, but he suspected it was more to show appreciation for his longevity than because they needed another manager.

A Wolf of His Own

The band, Wolf Party, didn't rehearse much, they had
a number of big band songs along with hits from the
1960s and 70s in their repertoire. All the members were
talented, classically trained musicians. Dean was on
drums, he was brilliant but chronically ran late—he kept
excellent time, so they forgave him. Kelly was on
keyboards and sometimes guitar, depending on what the
song needed. She was very focused and tended not to
stick around after shows. Emma was on bass; she'd
mastered Larry Graham's slap bass technique in her mid-
teens and liked to show off. The last two members of the
band were his cousins, fraternal twins Jeremy, on lead
guitar, and Ingrid who was their lead singer.

Patrice, the owner of Jack's Bar and Roman's boss,
was very generous about the band arrangements.
Occasionally there would be a local rock band, or some
touring group, who would take the headline spot, and if
not, Wolf Party would do two or sometimes three sets on
their own. The crowd weren't vocal fans, but they'd get
up and dance to the more popular numbers.

Roman rolled over and snoozed the alarm on his
phone; it was just gone three in the afternoon, and he
needed to get started on his day soon to avoid rushing to
be at work on time. Sometimes it felt as though his life
disappeared into late nights at the bar, but he supposed it
was better for his cool musician image if he was mostly
nocturnal.

When the alarm went off again ten minutes later, he
was awake enough to check if any messages or
notifications had come through before letting his eyelids

slide closed again. Nothing from that nice young police officer, which was a pity.

*

Roman arrived at the bar at six that evening. Wolf Party's first set started at seven, and they had to make sure the stage was set up before the bar got too crowded. The bar served food, and though they weren't known for their dining experience, it was always good to have a few items on the menu to stop people from getting too drunk too quickly. It also didn't hurt that having food meant people headed into the bar earlier, increasing their takings overall. He was careful whenever Patrice wanted advice on how to run the business that he didn't suggest anything too strongly. She was just as likely to put him in charge of anything he brought up, and the kitchen was an area he wanted to stay out of. With the band and managing the bar several nights a week, he wasn't looking to spend any more time at Jack's.

The place was about half full. The young people who drank there on the weekend weren't out yet, and he figured they would likely be drinking at home to start and heading out after ten. Jeremy and Ingrid were there already, chatting to a group of people Roman didn't recognize. Roman turned his head sharply as he caught a whiff of a familiar scent; he could have sworn Jason was in the bar, but when he looked around he couldn't see the young man anywhere.

Wishful thinking. He checked his phone; still no contact. Perhaps he wasn't interested, or was working, or maybe he thought he had to wait a day or so to use the number so as not to seem too interested. Roman hated the dating game. He wanted more than anything to settle down with someone, to skip the uncertainty of dating and go straight to a nice, secure relationship, but he knew that wasn't the way things worked.

"Earth to Roman?" Jeremy said, playfully punching him in the arm.

"Sorry, I was miles away. What were you saying?"

"I was asking how you are, dufus. I haven't seen you around since last weekend's gig."

"Oh, yeah. I didn't come to the family dinner last Sunday. Patrice needed me to cover the Sunday night shift."

"Your mother wasn't happy you weren't there." Jeremy raised his eyebrows meaningfully.

"I know. She gave me an earful the next day. All about the importance of family, and keeping the traditions alive and all that. Sometimes life gets in the way, you know?"

"I know, but my mom isn't the head of the Council."

"You're gonna have to make it up to her tomorrow," Ingrid said, butting into the conversation. "Jer is right, she was really mad."

Roman sighed. "Well, that's tomorrow's problem." He spotted Dean struggling to bring some of his gear in through the door at the back of the bar, and went to help, thankful for the opportunity to get away from his cousins and their reminder that he'd let his mom down.

"Thanks, bro." Dean handed him a large drum box. It was only twenty minutes after their arranged meeting time, early for Dean who was often thirty or forty minutes late.

"How've you been?" Roman asked, as they took the gear up to the stage.

"Same old stuff, you know how it is. Your mom was real cut up about you missing family dinner though. I thought she was gonna rip someone's throat out right there."

"It's not the first time I've missed a dinner." Roman squeezed the bridge of his nose. If he'd realized how much shit he'd get for skipping the meal, he might have told Patrice he couldn't cover the shift or tried to do both.

"Yeah, I know, but it's heading towards Lammas and she wants you to stand for the Council." Dean was a distant relation, and though Roman wasn't sure how their bloodlines merged, every member of the Wolf Party was part of the weekly family dinners that his mom hosted. It was a massive undertaking, with thirty or forty people each time, but since Vanessa had become the head of the Council a decade or so before, she had insisted on regular meetings. Most of the members came a couple of times a month, but as her son, he was expected at every dinner.

"Lammas isn't for weeks, and I've said no to being on the Council for years. Why is it different now?"

"Because there's a spot opening up, and… I dunno, man, she's your mother, shouldn't you know the answer to that?"

Roman rolled his eyes and got back to setting up the drum kit. Jeremy left with Dean to get the remaining gear, and Ingrid came over to help with the kit stands.

"Aunt Vanessa says she wants you to fulfill your destiny. The leadership of our pack has always been in the family, and with my dad stepping down this year, she wants you to fill the gap."

Roman sighed. "I'm not political. I don't want to be in charge of the pack. I don't know what I want to do with my life, but it feels like it's all been planned out by Mom…"

"No one wants to think their life is being run by their mother, but she has a point. You've got natural leadership skills, you're the most powerful wolf in the pack, except for her and dad. Plus, it's not just politics, it's about keeping us safe. Without the Council, we risk being hunted or worse."

Roman didn't like to think about his obligations to the pack. He'd been born into the dynasty of powerful leaders of wolf shifters in San Destino. Their whole pack took direction from Vanessa, who kept them in check. She made sure there were no accidental shiftings, and they'd kept fatalities down to zero for years under her leadership. He didn't like to think about stepping into her shadow and failing. He wasn't sure how long he would be able to hold her off, especially with his uncle stepping down from leadership. He was a powerful wolf, but his political talents left a lot to be desired. The constant fighting with his sister wasn't helping either.

"Anyway, you have to go tomorrow. I'm not defending you to her two weeks in a row. It's not worth my life if she thinks you're up to something."

"I'm not up to something, I had to work here. Patrice had no one to run the bar—"

"I know, you said that, but you know Vanessa doesn't care about Normie business. Pack business always takes precedence."

"You're right. I'll go." He had hoped to try to find Jason tomorrow night, maybe go on a nice date, but damage control with his mother on the warpath was more important than a sexy boy he'd met last night. There would be plenty of time to find him and work out whether it was lust or something more.

*

Jason slept late on Saturday morning. He didn't have to work for a few days, so he didn't even set an alarm. Since becoming a cop, his sleeping hours had been a mess. They had a twenty-four-hour rotating roster of ten-hour shifts. He often worked strange patterns, like four days on, four days off, which meant planning his social life and his sleep schedule was a skill he had yet to master. One of his TOs had said, "At some point your body learns to sleep whenever you lay down, but it could take a while."

He got up, went to the bathroom, and came back to look at the napkin the bartender had given him. He was pretty sure it was a name and number, what else would he have written there, but it had bled completely. All he could make out was the first letter of the name, which was either an R or a B, and the right number of smudges underneath to be a cell phone number. Jason smiled to himself. He didn't usually get any attention when he was out. Especially not when he was hanging out with his colleagues; they were highly effective at blocking any kind of interest he might show. Jack's was a nice place, but he didn't go there often due to the number of San Destino police employees who hung out there.

Maybe it was fate that the number had been washed away in the rain, but something about the bartender kept popping into his mind. A magnetism, some sort of animalistic heat, nothing Jason could put his finger on, but the smile that crept over his face when he thought about the smattering of dark chest hair peeking out of his shirt, of the arresting amber eyes, meant he wouldn't forget the strapping bartender any time soon.

I wish I remembered his name, Jason thought as he wandered into the kitchen. It was after midday, and his roommate, Holly, was out. He opened the fridge and stared at it hoping for inspiration. It didn't come. He let the door swing closed and made toast and coffee.

As he was slathering butter on his toast—which was slightly burned since Holly always turned up the toaster—he thought about the bartender again.

What's a five-letter name beginning with R? Randy? Rider? No, that didn't sound right. Rowan? That's closer, but not quite right. Jason could picture the guy's name tag in his mind, but it wasn't clear. If only he had an eidetic memory, it would really come in handy for his work as well as for remembering the names of cute boys.

Roman, that fits much better.

"What are you grinning at?" Holly asked. Jason startled, almost dropping the knife he'd been using to butter his toast.

"Where did you come from? I thought you were out."

"I was on the porch, but you were off in la-la-land, I'm not surprised you didn't see or hear me. So come on, spill—who's got you looking all wistful?"

"No one." Jason wasn't ready to share Roman with anyone yet.

"Uh huh. I don't believe it, but if you don't want to share, then I can't make you."

He didn't think she'd let it drop, but maybe she was feeling generous.

"What are you doing today anyway?"

"Nothing planned… why?" He wondered if she was letting the wistful look go because she wanted something.

"I need to go to the mainland, gotta see someone about a class I'm thinking of taking…"

"On the mainland?" People didn't leave San Destino much, so it must be some course if she was looking to go across the bridge to get there.

"Yeah, it's a hand-carving woodwork one. The teacher's coming up from Los Angeles, and my sister was supposed to come with me, but she's got a head cold or something. So, I want company."

Jason took a bite of toast to buy himself some time to think. He had no plans, and he didn't have a shift until Tuesday; he could afford to do something spontaneous. He had half been considering going to the bar to ask for Roman's number again, but on a Saturday night they'd be swamped. "What time is this class?"

"Starts at two, goes for four hours. We could even grab dinner before we come back."

"And I don't have to pay you back for the ticket?"

"Nope, all paid for."

She really was laying it on, and dinner as well. "Alright," he glanced at the clock, "I'll get dressed and be ready to go in like, ten minutes."

"EEE," Holly squealed and clapped her hands. "It's going to be so great!"

*

The woodworking class was challenging and excellent fun. Holly got really into it, but Jason kept thinking there was something he'd forgotten. He always felt strange on the mainland, like his mind was cloudy or he'd left the oven on. They got back after dark, and he went straight to bed.

He had intended on going right to sleep, but his mind was working overtime wondering what Roman was up to and whether he'd noticed Jason hadn't texted. Then he started to wonder if he was even serious, or just after a roll in the hay. Someone as hot as Roman would have his choice of partners, and being a bartender was an aphrodisiac to most people, whereas being a cop seemed to be a turn off.

Jason had tried online dating, but San Destino was a pretty small city, and he worried that someone would see him there and tell his colleagues before he was ready. He also didn't fancy hooking up with most of the guys who were on those apps; despite having a healthy libido, he didn't much like sex with strangers. It always felt like a let down.

At some point he must have fallen asleep, even though it seemed like hours he was lying there, equal parts fantasizing and catastrophizing about his chances with Roman. As he looked at the pattern of early morning light on the ceiling, he decided he would go to the bar and ask Roman for his number again. Maybe he'd even be bold enough to ask for a date, though he suspected he would get all flustered and not be able to.

Holly was working that day. She was also a rookie cop with the SDPD, and on the afternoon shift, so he had the house to himself. He levered himself out of bed, threw on some clothes and went out to get a coffee and a bakery treat from around the corner. On Sundays, the produce market was always thriving, and they had a fantastic coffee van that sold baked goods from Nina's bakery in Juniper Hollow.

It was only a couple of minutes' walk. The day was already warm, though it was nearly midday so it shouldn't have been surprising.

"Caramel latte, please, and a bear claw," he said to the young woman working the van. She seemed a little frazzled.

"No worries, hun." She took his money, gave him the pastry, and set about making his coffee.

"Caramel latte?" she said loudly when she was done. It was probably habit, but she needn't have bothered, there were no other customers at that time.

"Thanks, that's me." He took the coffee, the aroma hitting his nostrils like he'd already tasted it. "Been busy today?"

"A little. We get a lot of traffic between nine and eleven, but it's dropped off now."

"When did you get here?" he asked, taking a sip. The coffee was glorious, nutty, and sweet with that sugary hit of caramel he loved.

"About six-thirty. The stall holders love their caffeine too." She smiled, though her eyes were tired.

"I know what you mean. Thanks again." Jason walked away, saving his bear claw for when he got home. Since he started on the job, he'd learned the importance of making conversation with shop owners. Building rapport over a short period of time was a must have skill for a good police officer, and though he was on patrol now, he wanted to move up the ranks, so he could use his brain as a detective. They seemed so important in the station, always running around doing their own thing. Plus, they seemed more progressive than some of his patrol colleagues, from what he could see; Evans even had a ponytail, and he was a guy.

*

Sunday dinners were a big deal to the Eldritch family—the fact that Roman had missed one last week had put him in the bad books with his mother, and his father, who generally agreed with her, so he had to make a good show this week. The dinners had started out being just him, his sister, and his parents, when he was around ten. Later, his mother had invited his uncle and their family, but it wasn't until she was elected as the head of the Council that Vanessa started using Sunday dinners as community networking opportunities.

Roman resented having to be there. He didn't think his presence made any difference, but his mom insisted it did. He couldn't think of anything worse; the machinations of politics, keeping everyone happy while lying out of one side of your mouth was not his idea of a good time. And they were volunteers, so he wouldn't even get paid to do it.

"Mom," he said, trying to inject as much enthusiasm into his voice as possible, but failing.

"Roman, my boy. You made it." His mom managed to make it sound like a scolding without saying so.

"Yes, I'm here."

"You were missed last week. I wanted to talk to you about taking on your Uncle Bobby's position on the Council."

"Yeah, Jeremy and Ingrid filled me in."

"Did they. What do you think?"

"Can I help with anything?" Roman changed the subject. He'd arrived exactly on time, knowing most of the guests were late by nature, and that he would be roped into helping as soon as he arrived.

"You can help your father on the grill. And don't think I didn't notice you not answering my question."

"Okay." Roman hugged his mom with one arm before she swept away to greet someone else. The family home in Chapel Hill was one of San Destino's famous terrace houses. Painted in a loud dark red and mustard yellow color scheme on the outside, it had a much more understated style inside. He moved down the hallway and through the kitchen, depositing his light beers in the cooler as he did, and out the back onto the deck his dad had built a few summers ago.

"Dad." Roman nodded.

"Son." His father, Bryce, returned the nod. He wasn't a talkative man, Vanessa had always done enough talking for the both of them, and while he usually agreed with whatever she said, every so often he would stand his ground. It was a relief that someone could stand up to his mother, and that, miraculously she usually listened.

"Mom says you need a hand."

"She wants me to convince you to run for Bobby's Council spot."

"Ah." Roman twisted open the bottle of lager he'd brought with him.

"I said I'd mention it, so there I've mentioned it."

"Thanks." They were silent for a while, his father occasionally adjusting the food on the grill.

"You'd be good at it, y'know."

"What?" Roman asked.

"The Council."

"I'm not the least bit politically minded. I'm way too blunt for a start."

His father chuckled. "That's exactly what they need. Bobby's the voice of reason, the voice of the clan, and more importantly, a check on your mother to make sure she doesn't get too caught up in her grand plans and forget what she's supposed to be focusing on."

"I'm no good at standing up to Mom."

"You just need practice. Most of the time she's doing good work, but sometimes she gets in her own way, and the good intentions start getting lost in the ends justifying the means."

Roman had never paid much attention to the way the wolf shifter Council operated, or how it fit in with the

Council of Elites of the San Destino, but perhaps he should get more interested. If he was to be there to keep things moving, and to stop his mother disappearing up her own behind, maybe there was something attractive about the role after all.

*

They all ate at the large metal table outside on the patio. The sun hung low in the sky, and the summer breeze was taking some of the heat from the day, but it was still hot. Bryce's grilled meats had gone down a treat, and there were only scraps of salad and a few bread rolls left.

"Help me clear away, will you, Roman?" Vanessa said. Roman stood and collected plates from around the table, while his sister, Connie, sat nursing her third beer.

Back in the kitchen, his mother had put a pile of plates next to the sink and waved for him to do the same. When she caught sight of his expression, she frowned.

"What are you sulking about?" she asked.

"Nothing."

"Tell that to your face." The words were delivered as a joke, but he didn't feel like having this conversation again.

"Next time, ask Connie to help. You never make her clean up."

Vanessa's eyebrows rose and she pursed her lips. "I invite you to my home, cook for you, and this is your attitude to lending a hand?"

Dad did most of the cooking, Roman thought. "It would be nice if we took it in turns. I clean up after people all day at work, I don't want to do it when I'm supposed to be out having a nice time." He didn't know why he was getting so worked up about it; it wasn't a big deal in the scheme of things, but something about his parents trying to get him to join the Council, had initially seemed interesting but now felt like a chore; like he was being saddled with all the roles of responsibility and Connie had none.

"First, I didn't bring you up to spend your life keeping score of who has done what; if you see something that needs doing, you do it. Second, this isn't just a night out for you, this is family and family comes with obligations."

"For me, sure. I'll believe it when I see Connie having anywhere near the obligations I get stuck with."

Vanessa's frown deepened and she took two steps towards him. "You are the older brother, and you are the eldest male in your generation—quite apart from which your sister and cousins don't have the same… aptitudes you do, and I can't rely on them like I do with you."

"Is that what getting me on the Council is for then? So you can palm off a bunch of stuff to me and let everyone else off the hook?"

Vanessa shook her head. "You need to think about your words before letting them out of your mouth. I'm your mother, and your pack leader. When I ask you for something, you should be asking what else can I do, not trying to get something out of it for yourself. If you're going to be that ungrateful, you can leave right now."

Roman stood, dumbfounded for a moment. His mother hadn't been so direct with him since before he left home. Something about this whole situation felt wrong, but he couldn't put his finger on it. Whatever was happening, he'd had enough of it.

"Fine, I'm leaving. I don't need this." He walked to the front door and left his parents' house without a backwards glance. As soon as he was outside, walking in the balmy night air, it felt as though he could breathe again. Something had put him off his game; usually he could hold his resentments and jealousies in while he visited his parents, but tonight there was nothing left in the tank—he just let it all get to him, and as he walked, his regret grew.

The rest of the pack, and most of his generation, his sister and cousins, all thought being a wolf shifter was the best thing about their personalities. They loved to go up to the hills, shift into their wolf forms, and run around in the moonlight, like it was some great adventure, but Roman avoided shifting. Ever since the string of maulings a couple of years ago, which turned out to be a bear shifter who had lost control of his abilities, Roman had been frightened of the kind of damage he could do if he lost control in his wolf form.

He hadn't been heading anywhere in particular when he left his parents' place, but he found himself approaching Providence Pier. It was still busy; people were walking along the foreshore hand in hand, gazing out over the water or into one another's eyes, and he was reminded that the cute police officer from the other night hadn't called him yet. The rejection stung.

Roman thought he caught a whiff of Jason's scent, then shook his head—wishful thinking. He sighed and turned to walk home. He needed sleep, maybe a beer first and some TV.

"Hey uhh—"

Fast footsteps came towards him and he turned. Jason was waving his arm and trying to catch up. Roman stood and waited for the other man to arrive.

"Hey, um, thanks for stopping."

"It's good to see you again." Roman's voice was deep and gravelly. The scent of Jason in his nostrils unfurled a desire in his belly.

"I…" Jason's cheeks were flushed, and he looked away. "I was going to call you, but I was caught in the rain on my way home, the note got wet, and I couldn't make out the number, or your name, and then when I went to the bar to try to find you, they said you were off. I nearly gave up, thought the universe must be sending me a sign, but then there you were."

Roman watched the smaller man, his hands gripped each other nervously, struggling to maintain eye contact. There was a tiny undercurrent of fear in his scent, probably fear of rejection, but perhaps a little part of him was afraid of what would come next if not. Jason seemed so innocent.

"My name is Roman."

Jason sighed. "Jason."

"I know." Roman couldn't help the predatory purr in his voice. Something about how flustered Jason was really turned him on. They stood in silence for a moment. Roman took the time to look at his companion, while Jason fidgeted.

"Could I have your number again? I'll put it straight into my phone this time." Jason looked into his eyes for a moment, and there was hunger there. Despite his nervous exterior, he knew what he wanted.

"On one condition," Roman said.

"Uh, sure."

"I'll give you my number in exchange for a kiss."

Jason's eyes widened briefly in surprise. "Alright, that seems fair."

Roman took a step closer, the gap between them now much too narrow to be platonic. The heat coming off Jason's body was intense, and his energy was frantic. He smelled desire under the apprehension, and Jason took a half-step forward. They weren't quite touching, but there was barely an inch between them.

He slipped one hand onto Jason's hip, the other went to his neck, as Roman lowered his mouth to Jason's. He was taking his time; the agonizing slowness of the moment was torturous but delightful and gave Jason the time to pull away if he didn't want to kiss him.

Jason's breathing was shallow, head tilted up, but Roman lingered just out of reach, hoping Jason would close the gap. After what felt like a long time, Jason brought his lips to meet Roman's and the yearning he'd been trying to keep in check rushed over him. The kiss started tenderly, but Roman pulled Jason's body against his, pressing their mouths together urgently.

Jason responded by wrapping his arms around Roman's torso and deepening the kiss. He lost all sense of time as they stood there at the entrance to the pier, in full view of everyone, and kissed as though it was their last chance. In the end, the itch between his shoulder blades, the sense people were watching, made Roman pull away first. Jason's eyes stayed closed for a moment, and when he opened them, he seemed confused.

"People are looking," Roman said, his voice low. Jason looked around him, and a few people turned away, caught in the act.

"Oh no. I…" he stumbled over his words. "My colleagues at the station don't know I'm gay."

Roman cocked an eyebrow. "Does that matter?"

"I don't know."

"I don't recognize any of the people watching, or on the pier. I don't think it will be a problem, but…"

"I'm sorry, I'm usually so cautious about meeting new people, but I couldn't help it."

"I know what you mean. That was some kiss."

Jason's cheeks flushed again. "You owe me a phone number now."

"Of course," Roman said, smiling. He felt giddy, like a teenager with a crush. He read out his number, while Jason stored it on his phone.

"I was going to suggest that we grab a beer and sit on the beach, but maybe not if you're feeling exposed."

"A beer sounds nice, if you agree to no more public displays."

Roman smiled. "I'll resist the temptation if you do."

Chapter 3

Walking along the pier next to Roman without touching him was almost impossible. Jason shoved his hands into his jeans pockets to quell the urge to hold his hand. Roman had seemed fine with the public display, it was his hang-up about someone from work seeing him that was the issue, so he couldn't initiate anything now he'd told Roman not to.

They walked past Jack's Bar and stopped into the new place Lovebirds instead. Jason assumed he didn't want to hang out in the bar where he worked, especially for what he hoped was a date. Lovebirds was busy, but subdued. People were sitting with beers, or brightly colored cocktails, and a few were still eating. They took a spot at the back, in a dark corner, and Roman ordered a couple of red wines.

"I'm glad I ran into you. I know it was only a couple of days ago, but I was starting to wonder if I'd read the vibe wrong," Roman said, leaning in, his voice low and sultry. Jason shivered. If only he didn't care about people seeing them, he would have turned to kiss those full, dark lips.

"I… uh… you didn't read my vibe wrong. I wasn't sure if you meant it when you handed me that napkin. I didn't look while I was with my colleagues. Being a rookie means they find something to tease me about all the time, but I didn't need them noticing that."

"I'm sorry it made you uncomfortable. It bothers me when people are rude to their employees—and I don't mean friendly banter, a bit of teasing here and there is fine, but what I saw was more like bullying and it made it hard for me to think clearly."

Jason flicked his eyes up to look at Roman, he seemed almost embarrassed. "I'm glad you did. I would never have been brave enough to ask for your number. I…" he broke off.

"What?"

He hesitated. "I thought you were into women."

Roman smiled, then chuckled, a low hearty sound from deep in his chest. It sent ripples of arousal through Jason and he had to squeeze his hands together to keep from reaching out to touch Roman's hand. "I don't like to label myself, but let's just say I've been with people of all genders."

Jason smiled and looked away. There was something hungry in his eyes, a burning desire for him that felt almost overwhelming; exciting, but a little scary.

"What about you?"

"Oh, umm." Jason stopped, as the server brought them their wines. "Thanks," he said, waiting until she'd walked away. "I don't really know. I haven't been with many people, but they've all been men."

Roman grinned, that hungry sparkling in his eyes again, and took a sip of his wine. "Good thing we sorted that out before we got too much further. I wouldn't want my kissing you to be misunderstood. I think you're hot, Jason, and I would like to see where that takes us."

Jason resisted the urge to giggle. "I think you're hot too. Wow, I never say that sort of thing out loud, especially to the person I'm talking about, and I haven't even had any of this wine."

They chatted, flirting outrageously for an hour or so, while studiously maintaining a gap between his body and Roman's, before the Lovebirds staff started cleaning up.

"I guess they want us to leave soon," Jason said.

"Yeah. Looks like it's closing time." Roman looked deep into Jason's eyes, and he had to look away. The heat building in Jason's belly was hard enough to control already. "Would you like to continue this somewhere else?"

"Uh…" Jason hesitated.

"I mean, we can always call it for tonight. You have my number now, and you know where I work."

"I'd like to see you again, maybe somewhere quieter." Jason shifted in his seat. Maybe he needed to man up and accept that if he wanted to date and not have to worry constantly about a colleague seeing him, he should just tell them.

"Sure, what if I make you dinner at my place?"

"That would be fantastic," Jason said, his mind already turning over what it meant to have their second date at Roman's and wondering what he looked like under his tight polo shirt. "Let me get the drinks, if you're making dinner."

"Alright," Roman said, standing to leave. His hand twitched and Jason wondered if he had intended to take his hand and changed his mind. Another reason to get over his hang-up about being affectionate in public.

*

Picking a time they were both off work for dinner was easier said than done—Roman had Wednesday off, but that was Jason's first day back on shift, and he was on nights this week starting at 10pm so they had settled on Monday the following week.

It felt like an age since he'd seen Roman, smelled his musky, spicy scent, but Jason was sure the wait would be worth it. He stood outside Roman's sharehouse in Bloomington and rubbed his sweaty palms on his jeans. He checked the time, took a deep breath, and pressed the doorbell.

Roman opened the door almost immediately, and Jason took half a step back in surprise.

"Hey, sexy. Come in." Roman stepped back to allow him inside. The front door opened onto the living room, with two squishy-looking corduroy sofas and a massive TV along one wall. There were bookshelves, which looked as though they'd seen better days, full of scruffy paperbacks and an assortment of knick-knacks and sports memorabilia. The combination of items struck Jason as incongruous.

"I live with three other guys. Each of us puts our stuff wherever it fits and as a result the décor is somewhat schizophrenic." He chuckled.

"How did you know I was thinking that?"

"Because everyone thinks that when they walk in here." Roman took Jason's hand and stepped close. He could feel the heat of his body, and the scent of his cologne filled his senses. "All my roommates are out, in case you're wondering."

Jason squeezed his hand. "So, we're all alone?"

"Yep. We have a system where if one of us needs the house for something, usually a hot date, the others will make themselves scarce. We've got a couple of hours completely alone." The hungry look in Roman's eyes was back, and he was staring at Jason's lips.

"In that case…" Jason closed the gap between them, tilted his face up and kissed Roman. If he was surprised, he recovered quickly—the kiss moved from tender to fiery.

Their bodies pressed against one another. Roman's body emanated heat in a way Jason hadn't encountered before. He wanted to be closer, to feel Roman's skin against his, and he slipped his hands under his navy collared shirt to feel the silky smooth skin over his obliques, before encountering the covering of hair over his stomach. Roman twitched a little at the touch, tilted his head back, and he sighed.

Jason kissed the exposed portions of his neck, his lips thrilling over the stubble there. Roman made a sound deep in his throat, somewhere between a growl and a purr, before grabbing Jason's waist, walking him backwards and pressing him against the wall of the entrance way.

"I could just eat you," Roman said, thrusting his leg between Jason's thighs.

"I'd let you," Jason said, with a small moan.

"Should we eat, first?" Roman pulled away a little, his breath ragged.

"What?"

"I mean, it's hardly gentlemanly to pounce on you as soon as you walk in the door."

Jason could feel his hard-on through his jeans where Roman's pelvis was still pressed into his own. "I, uhh…" Jason's brain was filled with Roman's scent. The only thing he could think about was ripping his clothes off and licking him all over.

"Unless, you want to continue… this?" There was a sparkle in Roman's eye, and he thought he must be teasing him.

"I don't mind you not being a gentleman just this once. We really should finish what we've started." Jason tried to match his energy, hoping there was a cheeky sparkle in his gaze.

"Mmm," Roman said, driving his body against Jason's again, kissing him as though with his whole body. "Come with me."

*

Roman took Jason's hand and led him upstairs, his body thrumming with desire. Jason followed but faltered as they crossed the threshold of the bedroom.

"Are you okay?" Roman turned back, Jason had turned pale.

"I, uh…"

Roman tilted his head to the side and waited for Jason to go on.

"I haven't been in anyone's bedroom for a while."

Roman smiled. "It's just a room. We don't have to do anything if you don't want to."

"I do want to. I'm just…"

"Nervous?" he said. Jason nodded. Roman stepped beside him and stroked his cheek. "It can be weird sometimes, maybe for no reason. How about we sit on the bed and see how we feel?"

Jason nodded. Roman sat on the edge of the bed and patted the space next to him. Jason sat, a little further away than he might have expected, given the hungry way he had been kissing him earlier. Roman turned to him, his hand resting on Jason's thigh, gently rubbing up and down. His hard-on had subsided since the mood shifted, but it wouldn't need much to come back strong.

Roman had been with a lot of people of all genders. Sometimes, he wondered if it was becoming blasé, but he knew nothing of Jason's history.

"Do you want to talk about it?"

"I…" Jason shifted closer and stared straight ahead. "I had experiences in college, just one-time things, you know. I've done a little bit since I came back home, but this feels different. I don't know if I'm making sense."

"Whatever you're feeling is valid. I think you're really hot, but I'm not in any rush. We can go back downstairs, have dinner, and see how you feel later."

Jason took a deep breath as though building up to something, then turned and kissed him gently. Roman understood he wanted to be guided, slowly unfolded like a flower, not ravaged.

They kissed tenderly, and Roman guided them back so they were lying on the bed, facing one another. He wriggled closer and put his leg over Jason's hip. He ran his fingertips over Jason's arms, and up under the sleeve of his shirt. Jason sighed, and snuggled in, their bodies flush against one another. Roman let out a small moan.

He glided his hand down Jason's back and pressed him further into his body. He felt so good, smelled so good, but there was something skittish about him tonight.

"Shall we get more comfortable?" Roman asked. Their legs were still dangling off the side of the bed. Jason nodded.

Roman shifted up onto the bed, toeing his shoes off and pulling his shirt over his head. Jason hesitated briefly, then did the same, scooching up next to him on the pillows.

When they resumed kissing, there was a little more urgency for both of them, being skin to skin heightened his arousal. Roman found himself grinding his thigh against Jason's groin, which resulted in another small sigh.

Emboldened, Roman started to kiss Jason's neck, reveling in the feel of his smooth skin. He kissed across the clavicle, and down Jason's pecs, brushing his lips over the nipple and eliciting another sigh. His mouth hovered over the blond trail of hair coming from the top of Jason's jeans, looking back up to his face.

"Is this okay?" He was breathless with desire. Jason nodded.

Roman unbuckled Jason's jeans, pushing them, and his underwear down to expose his glorious, pale, smooth, rock-hard cock. Jason tensed briefly and Roman waited for the small nod to continue.

Roman stroked Jason's cock, feather-light strokes on the sensitive underside, and slid his body back up so he was face to face with his lover. Ever so slowly, he increased his pressure, then wrapped his hand around Jason's cock and started pumping slowly.

Jason's eyes closed and arched his back in response, his hips moving in time with Roman's hands. Then his eyes flew open, he shuddered and came.

"I'm so sorry, I didn't mean to."

Roman's hand slowed, going back to his feathering strokes. "Why are you sorry? It's a perfectly natural response to a super-hot man jerking you off." He kept his tone light.

Jason flushed. "I can do you—"

"Don't worry about me." The hard-on under his pants felt huge, but it would subside. Instead, Roman reached down and scooped up the cum on Jason's stomach, licking his fingers. "We've got time to give each other plenty of orgasms."

*

Jason lay back trying to get his breathing to return to a normal pace. He felt guilty for not giving Roman the pleasure he'd received, but he'd said no, and it wasn't his place to disagree.

He looked around the bedroom, taking in the details. It was large for a bedroom, a perk of living in one of the older style houses in San Destino, with a plaster ceiling rising above the frosted glass pendant light. The bedframe was an old-fashioned, solid black wrought iron, though the mattress was firm and comfortable. The bookshelves and wardrobe were similarly antique, and there was a gorgeous antique writing desk, though it was covered in an array of stuff including books, a laptop, and various hair and skin care products. Though the furniture looked curated, the walls were bare of art, which made the room look somehow unfinished.

"Did you buy all the antiques?"

"Hmm?" Roman's heated body was still pressed along his side.

"The furniture, did you buy it?"

"Oh, yeah. It started with the bed, which I inherited from a great-uncle, and then I thought I should make the rest of the stuff match. It's a work in progress."

"It's lovely." Jason looked down at the gorgeous naked body next to him; dense and muscular, covered in hair, it was exactly the way he thought a man should look. Not like his slim, hairless body. To his own mind, he looked like a teenager, not a grown man; he would never be as masculine as Roman. The men in his family were small and not very hirsute.

"What are you thinking?" Roman asked, perhaps seeing the frown that had crept over Jason's face.

"Nothing."

"You frown at nothing often?"

Jason's lips curled in a half-smile. "If you promise not to laugh at me, I'll tell you."

"I promise."

"I was just thinking how much I like your body and wondering what you see in mine. I'm sorry, it isn't really the time after well… you know."

"Hey," Roman looked up at him, his eyes clouded with concern. "Firstly, all bodies are amazing and deserve love. Secondly, yours in particular is very enticing—it's all smooth and taut, like a gymnast, eminently kissable, and bonus points for being a good size for me to pick up, if I were so inclined." As he spoke, the hungry look returned to his face, as though describing Jason had reminded him of all the things they'd just done.

"Thanks." Jason wanted to be reassured, clearly he was Roman's type, but though his mind heard the words, his heart didn't feel it. Roman's grin faltered a little.

"Shall we go down and have some dinner? Maybe if we're wearing clothes you might feel less, I dunno, exposed?"

Jason smiled. "Good idea."

*

Roman had tidied the kitchen before Jason's arrival specifically so that he would have everything he needed at his fingertips to make dinner.

"I've got steaks, and I thought we could have some baked potatoes and a green salad, if that seems good to you." Roman watched Jason, that insecurity that he thought was only because there were people around them the other night at the bar was back. He wondered how many people Jason had dated, and whether there was more to this shyness than youthful anxiety or inexperience.

"That sounds wonderful."

Roman wrapped the potatoes in foil and put them into the oven, then set about assembling the salad. "The potatoes will take a while, I'll give them half an hour then we can slap the steaks on the grill."

"Great."

"Would you like a beer while we wait? They're just in the fridge if you want to grab me one too," Roman said, chopping red bell peppers to go into the salad.

"Of course." He reached in and grabbed two of the bottles of beer and set one in front of Roman. The silence between them felt strained, and Roman worried he was being a bad host, unable to make his date feel settled in his home.

"What made you join the police? Are you from a police family?" he asked.

"No. My parents were surprised as well to be honest. My mom is a teacher, and Dad is a probate lawyer. They each thought I was going to do what they did, but when I didn't get into the college I wanted to, and I went to the community college just across the Destiny Bridge, they realized I wouldn't be following in their footsteps quite the way they wanted me to."

Roman suspected there was something underneath that comment about not getting into his preferred college, but decided it was a conversation for later, when they knew each other better. One of the skills he'd learned as a bartender over the years was when to push, and when to stay quiet. People would usually tell you what was on their mind if you gently asked questions and left space for their answers.

"What did you plan to do before that?"

"I had intended to be a criminal defense lawyer, helping people to make sure that one mistake didn't mean they'd ruined their lives. Plus, our sentences seem to be much longer than other Western countries, and worse if you're a person of color. I'm passionate about not punishing people for poverty; if stealing food is the only way to stop from starving, then should they go to prison? If the only way to get out of your neighborhood is to sell drugs on the corner, how do we help people to have other paths? You know what I mean?"

Roman's eyebrows raised. "I don't think I've ever met a cop with those particular values."

Jason laughed. "Yeah. My colleagues think I should be a social worker; call it a bleeding-heart mentality."

"I can see why you're hesitant for them to know about your personal life."

Jason looked away. "There are one or two people who know. Riley, my training officer, she's gay too, and she knows. She's so much stronger than me in that way, doesn't give a shit what people think about her."

Roman was quiet for a moment, grabbing the steaks and taking them out to the grill on the patio out the back. "Follow me."

It was a small wooden deck, about six by four feet, with a disproportionately large grill sitting on it, along with four folding chairs leaning against the wall. The house had a small patch of lawn beyond the deck, but since it was a sharehouse and none of them had a green thumb, the garden wasn't much to look at. He unfolded one of the chairs for Jason and indicated for him to sit.

Roman turned on the burners and put the steaks on before returning to the previous conversation. "What do you think your colleagues would do if it was widely known that you were dating a man?"

"You mean apart from mercilessly teasing me?"

"Yeah. Would they hurt your career prospects? Make it difficult to do your job? Undermine you in the field?"

Jason took a swig from his beer bottle. "It's hard to say. Riley doesn't publicize the fact she's with a woman, but it's not a secret. People treat her the same as anyone else, though she fits in as one of the boys. I think it would be harder for me."

Roman was silent.

"They call me Tink."

"Where did that come from?"

"My last name, Bell, that plus the fact I'm small, they call me Tinkerbell and usually it's just shortened to Tink. I hate it."

Roman nodded. "I can see that would be upsetting."

"But apart from some light hazing, you know, putting shaving cream in my boots, or leaving wands around my locker, I don't think they treat me differently in the field."

"That's a relief. I had started to worry they would allow you to be put into dangerous situations just because they were homophobic jerks, but I'm glad that's not the case." Roman chose his words carefully. He had always been suspicious of the hyper-masculine attitude of the police, and the conversation raised his hackles, but it was too soon in the relationship for him to get all overprotective. The wolf in him was growling, but he was conscious of keeping it all inside.

"I'm sure they would get bored of it eventually. Maybe the nickname would stick, but if I was out, then the next queer rookie might not be so mortified, or targeted."

"Cultures take time to change, and the more people in the group who are different, the easier it is for others to join." Roman turned the steaks, they were almost ready. "Are you hungry?"

"Definitely, the smell of grilling always sets my tastebuds going." Jason grinned. His eyes were still a little sad, perhaps the conversation had been too heavy for before dinner.

They ate inside at the kitchen table. Roman kept meaning to get a table for the outside area, but since he hardly ever had friends around, and it was usually only him and his roommates out there with beers, he'd never gotten around to it. The enormous outdoor entertaining area his parents had was something he hoped to have when he finally settled down with someone. He liked the idea of being someone who had barbecues and gatherings in the open air. Vanessa would definitely approve, since she wanted him to follow in her footsteps onto the Council.

"How did you get into bar work?" Jason said, breaking into his thoughts.

Roman chuckled. "I guess I fell into it. I wanted to be a professional musician for a long time, and I thought having a flexible job like bartending would help with that, but I'm not sure it's worked the way I had hoped. I mean, the only gigs we really get are at the bar where I work, and I have to be behind the bar before and after the gigs."

"Do you enjoy it?"

"I love it, working with people, chatting with strangers, and I love beer, especially when the reps from the suppliers come out, or a new local craft brewer wants to get us to stock their beers, it's great." He sighed.

"But?"

Roman looked up, this man was sharp. "But it feels like a placeholder. My mother wants me to follow in her footsteps, and I don't know if I'll be able to live up to her expectations."

"Mothers can be difficult. What does she do that you would follow?"

"It's … uh, hard to explain." Roman took a large bite from his potato and chewed it. He'd walked straight into that question. Jason was a Norm, a person living in San Destino who wasn't part of the paranormal world, and Paranorms like him weren't allowed to reveal the town's secrets to a Norm without Council permission. It had been a long time since he'd been so foolish. "She's the leader of our local community center. It's a thankless job with lots of politics, but she's always seemed a natural at it."

"And you don't think you're up to it?"

"I've been rebelling against following her path for years, and I was sure she'd given up on the idea, but the other week at our family dinner, she mentioned it and… I guess I feel like I need a new challenge, and I've been considering it."

"Your people skills are very good, I can attest to that, and I'm sure everything else you would pick up easily."

"You're kind to say so. I'll think about it some more. I don't need to make any decisions now."

Roman had been at his parents' again the night before, and while his mother hadn't mentioned anything, it was clear she'd been thinking about it. Even his dad seemed to be feeding him bits of what might have otherwise been gossip, except it was the sort of thing he would need to know if he were to join the Wolf Council.

"Have you got any big plans this week, Roman?" his sister Connie had asked.

"I'm having dinner with someone tomorrow, otherwise nothing much. How about you?"

"Oh, no. Don't think you're getting away with not telling me who this dinner date is with."

Roman sighed. He had hoped it would sound like a friend, but Connie knew all of his friends, and not naming his dinner companion no doubt piqued her interest. "His name is Jason, he's in the San Destino Police Department—"

"He's a cop?" She wrinkled her nose. "Don't tell me he's a Normie too."

"As a matter of fact, I think he is. He doesn't have any talents or connections to any of the Paranorm groups as far as I can see."

"You can't think it's a good idea to date someone who doesn't know you're a wolf. It's basically your whole personality, and if Mom and Dad get their way, you'll be taking over the Council and what would you tell him then?"

Roman was stunned, he hadn't thought his sister was so prejudiced, but here she was spouting the same conservative, separatist talking points he'd heard his whole life. Yes, there were rules about revealing the paranormal world in San Destino to those who weren't in it, but there were no laws that said you couldn't—you just needed permission from the Council. He knew of several mixed relationships between Norms and Paranorms, although now he thought about it, they were never particularly long lived.

"To be honest, I was mostly just enjoying talking to a really hot guy, and haven't immediately been planning our wedding and happily ever after." Roman's anger was rising, and Connie was skilled at pressing his buttons after a lifetime of trying to get under his skin.

"Whatever you say… but mark my words, this will come back to bite you later. Dump him now before you get too many feelings."

Roman looked up from his mostly empty plate to look at Jason. It was too late to avoid feelings; they'd only known each other a short time, but he was already starting to fall for this hopeful, bright, sexy man.

"What are you grinning at?" Jason asked, his eyes twinkling in amusement.

"Nothing, just enjoying the view."

In spite of his sister's disapproval, Jason made him feel safe, comforted, and was sexy as hell, and that was more than he could say for most of the people he'd dated lately. So what if she thought it was a mistake to date outside of the wolf community, it was his life, and while it might make things a bit more difficult, he wouldn't change Jason for anything.

Chapter 4

Over the weeks, Jason and Roman spent more time together, getting to know one another slowly, and working around their often-incompatible work schedules. They spent evenings talking, and the sex got better and better. Jason even experimented with taking control once or twice.

Every time he woke up next to Roman was a thrilling experience. As he slowly came to wakefulness, the first thing he registered was the body heat—Roman ran hot— then he noticed his scent, that clear, masculine smell that was a combination of his cologne, his soap, and his own deep musk.

As he became more and more aware, Jason's body started to respond, blood rushing to his groin and filling his brain with all the places he wanted to touch, all the things he wanted to do. It was very distracting, lying there next to his gorgeous man. He'd almost called Roman his boyfriend in his mind, and had to remind himself that they hadn't had the talk yet. They were just dating, and seeing how things went. But it was so hard when everything in Jason's brain was planning their future together; their quaint little house, Roman running the community center and Jason working his way up in the police, maybe even helping out at the center when he wasn't on shift. It was a domestic existence Jason hadn't dared to imagine for himself until now, and the idea that it could all be taken away in a moment put a cold ball of lead into his gut.

Roman sighed and pulled Jason closer to him. Roman was the big spoon, and he felt the morning erection pressing into his back. He moved against Roman's naked body, hoping to bring him out of his sleepy state and into morning sex.

Jason's fantasies were interrupted by his cell phone ringing—he had set it up so that when the station called it would ring loudly regardless of whether he'd put it on silent.

"Crap," he muttered, extricating himself from the bed, grabbing the phone and stepping into the hallway as quickly as he could before answering. "Bell speaking."

"Officer Bell, this is Dispatch. The Watch Commander is requesting you to come into the station as soon as possible."

"Uh, okay. Has something happened?" His brain was still fuzzy from sleep, but his day off seemed to have been canceled.

"You'll be briefed when you get in. What's your ETA?" The dispatcher was a no-nonsense older woman who reminded him of his primary school teacher mother.

"Um…" He tried to make some mental calculations. He had a uniform at the station, though it was his spare, and if he got it soiled, he wouldn't have anything to change into. If he went home to change before he went in, it would take at least forty minutes, but if he went straight from Roman's, he could probably be there in fifteen. "Is it urgent?"

"It's best if you can be here as soon as possible, we have a time sensitive situation."

Jason ran his hand over his face. "I'll be there in fifteen minutes, twenty at the outside."

"Thanks, Bell." She hung up without further pleasantries. Jason assumed she was calling in everyone who wasn't on shift. He had time for a very quick shower but would have to postpone all of the sexy plans he had for the day. He slipped back into the bedroom as quietly as he could.

"Who was that?" Roman said, regarding him from the bed.

"Work. I have to go in."

Roman raised an eyebrow, and propped himself up on one elbow. "Your face looks like it's serious."

"They didn't give me any details over the phone, so I have to assume it is. Usually if someone's called in sick, they tell you."

"How serious?" Roman frowned.

"I won't know till I get there for the briefing, but if they're calling in people who are off duty, it's gotta be something big. Terror threat or a mass casualty event."

"Shit."

"Yeah. I need to get going. Can I quickly shower before I go?"

Roman smiled, his eyes crinkling. "You can shower, if I can come with you."

"I really can't let you, as appealing as that sounds."

"I guess I shouldn't get in the way of your duty, Officer." Roman sighed theatrically, but was still smiling. If they were going to be in a relationship, he would have to get used to the canceled plans.

*

Jason was at the San Destino Police Station in just under twenty minutes and was waved into the briefing room. The Watch Commander was seated at the front, along with half a dozen other officers who all looked harried. He spotted Riley sitting at one of the far tables and took a seat next to her. Her face was clouded with worry.

"Do you know what's going on?" he asked.

She waved her hand in a shushing motion as Ward stood up to address the group.

"You've all been pulled in because of a specific threat we've received. The detectives who have been looking into the significant vehicle incident on the Destiny Bridge back in March, have uncovered evidence of a drug trafficking operation being run out of a house in Chapel Hill. This may or may not be connected to the bridge incident."

A murmur went around the room. Chapel Hill was an expensive and respectable neighborhood, not the sort of place they were usually called into for drug busts.

"The information indicates that there will be a large shipment heading out of this house, where the substance is processed, later today, and we'll need to provide plain clothes support to the detectives and the uniformed officers who would usually be on duty," Ward continued. Jason looked at Riley, who was frowning at the Watch Commander.

"You'll be given individual assignments when you're in position, but for now, head over towards the coffee shop on Crest and Grant Street, and try to look inconspicuous. You'll need to be ready to go as soon as everyone is in place, and the detectives give the go ahead." Ward paired the officers off, assigning Jason to Riley, something he was glad of.

"What did we pull you away from?" Riley asked as they strolled out of the sliding doors at the front of the station. He felt strangely naked, not wearing the usual equipment belt, as he was out of uniform, though he had pepper spray, a taser and his service weapon in a backpack, along with his badge. The station wasn't far from the coffee shop, about a ten minute stroll, and they hadn't been allocated a vehicle.

"Uh, nothing really." He felt his cheeks redden.

"Nothing really?" she repeated. He glanced at her, and she seemed amused by his discomfort.

"I was at my boyfriend's place. Actually, we haven't talked about that yet, but you know what I mean."

Riley smiled. "I wondered if you were seeing someone. You seemed perkier lately. Good for you. Wanna talk about it?"

"It's early days still, I don't want to jinx it."

"Alright, Bell, whatever you say." She chuckled. "You haven't dated much, have you?"

They entered the coffee shop, ordered and took a seat at a table with a good view of the street.

"I've dated a bit, but I'm not what you'd call good at it. I've had a couple of relationships that lasted a month or two, nothing serious. Nothing that felt like this."

Riley put her hand on his shoulder. "That's great. I'm glad you've got someone special."

"Since you and Petra have been together you've really seemed to, I dunno, mellow or something."

"Are you saying I was harsh?"

"No, I just mean there's a settled quality about you that you didn't have. I want that for myself, you know?"

"Yeah, I know." She sipped her black coffee. "But you're still young and you've got plenty of time to meet your special someone and settle down, so try not to put pressure on yourself."

"You're probably right."

"Course I'm right." She looked out the window and frowned.

"What?"

"Nothing, just—" Riley's phone started to ring on the table. "Yes?" She listened and nodded before hanging up. "We gotta go."

Jason wondered what had caught her eye out the window, but there wasn't time to think about it now.

*

Roman had the day off work, and when Jason had been called in earlier his plans of lounging in bed together were dashed. He stared at the ceiling for a while, trying to find sleep, but it didn't come. He wondered what Jason was doing, it must have been something juicy for them to call him in on a day off. From what he knew, the police department avoided paying overtime when possible.

He got up, showered and dressed in light blue jeans and a tight black T-shirt, before making himself coffee and cereal for breakfast.

The idea of doing more for the community, and for the Wolf Council, had grown on him in the last few weeks. He'd avoided it for a long time, but his mother was an important figure and he wanted to support her and try to keep her from getting carried away with her grand schemes.

What would she be doing today? On a Tuesday, she would be at the community center in Zephyr Rise, west of the family home in Chapel Hill. Maybe he could drop in there and see what she did day-to-day. He hadn't ever paid too much attention to her day job, and he assumed it was part of taking on a role in the Council.

Roman walked the twenty minutes or so from his place to the community center and arrived a little after eleven o'clock. The center often had events on the weekends and sometimes networking or other community gatherings on weekdays. If he was going to eventually take on the role of leader of the pack, he'd need to get a handle on the center's activities and the pressure points in the community.

The Lupin Center had been established in the nineteen sixties, a period when the wolf shifter pack had been very politically active among the Elite Council. It was a period of unrest where some in the Elite Council wanted to stop all the secrecy and separation of Paranorms and

Norms, but in the end it was decided to keep the status quo. His maternal grandfather, Lloyd Eldritch, had been the pack leader at the time, he sided with those who wanted to be open in the community, and set up the center as a place to freely gather and support anyone who might be facing hard times. They did work in after school programs, arts and crafts, history and heritage classes, and they employed a social worker part-time who was available to help anyone who needed it.

The building was much older than the center, built around the turn of the twentieth century and featuring striking gothic wrought iron scrollwork on the front façade. It looked intimidating, until you saw the pieces of colored paper plastered all over the windows made by the kids who attended classes. When Roman walked in, the knitting and crocheting group were packing up—a chatty group of mostly older women he'd known since he was a child.

"Roman Eldritch," exclaimed a plump, smiling, middle-aged woman. "I don't think I've seen you in this place for years, at least not unless it's a special occasion."

"Hey, Meg. Yeah, I haven't been in for a while, busy with work, you know."

Meg raised an eyebrow. "Many of us make time for our community and charity work on top of work and family. But perhaps you're starting to take things like that more seriously, if the rumors are to be believed."

Roman rolled his eyes theatrically. "There are rumors already?"

"Oh yes, we've been waiting for the day you start taking your destiny seriously. There isn't a bet set up on it, but it was mentioned." She stood and slipped her arm into his. "Let's find your mother, she won't believe me if I tell her you're here without proof."

Roman wasn't a fan of Meg's response to his arrival, but he supposed a bit of skepticism and ribbing after having rejected the center so strongly through his teens and early twenties was to be expected. Growing up as the next in line to be pack leader was a pressure he'd always hated.

They walked down the narrow corridor behind the large main room towards the administration offices at the back, where Vanessa was working.

"Look who I found," Meg said.

"Roman? I didn't know you were dropping by, did I?" Vanessa asked.

"No, it was a last-minute decision." He smiled, hoping he would be greeted with warmth and no suspicion.

"Fantastic, I'm glad to see you. We have a few people referred to us by the Elite Council coming in for lunch. I'm sure we can stretch the catering to one more plate."

Roman was intrigued by the idea that the Elite Council would refer people to the center, given they were not always aligned in their goals.

"I'll take him from here, Meg," Vanessa said, and the other woman bobbed her head and walked back out. Vanessa beckoned him into the room. "Close the door, would you?"

He did as she asked and took a seat in front of her desk, which was covered in an array of papers.

"The Council asked that we look after a few people who are in a bit of trouble. They're not wolves, and I tried to push back and say we were already struggling to cater to the people we already have, but I was overruled. Also, your father said it would be good if we did them a favor; we could ask for one from them later. Anyway, they're a family of panther shifters, a mother and three young ones, new to San Destino after leaving a violent relationship with the father."

Roman nodded solemnly. He had no idea if this was the sort of client that was normal for the center, or alarming. He really was out of touch. "Is it a secret?"

"Not as such, but the fewer people who are aware of the exact details the better. And you know, Meg can't keep anything to herself." His mother smiled, though her eyes remained troubled.

"I know what you mean. So this isn't something you've done before? Helping shifters, I mean."

"We've done our fair share of political back scratching, and of course sometimes it's us who are asking, but no, this is the first time I've used the Center's resources for a favor like this."

Roman nodded. His head was swimming. He was a little disappointed in himself that he hadn't seen all the work his mother had been putting in—he supposed that was his own fault for prioritizing his job at Jack's and his music for the last few years. On the other hand, he was young, only twenty-six, and why shouldn't he have some carefree years before taking on the responsibility of leadership, something he was sure he would have to do.

"But that's not why you came to visit us, is it? Was there something you wanted?" His mother's shrewd eyes were trained on him, and he shifted a little under her scrutiny.

"I've just been thinking about what you and Dad said about being involved with the Wolf Council."

Vanessa nodded.

"I thought, since my plans for today fell through, I would see what you do, you know, day-to-day..."

It was a silly idea, no doubt his mother would send him away with a lecture about being a spectator in her life.

"I'm glad to hear you've been thinking about it. I hoped you'd reached an age where service to your community might be something you could make time for, but it was your father who really pushed for it. What were the plans that fell through?"

He had hoped she wouldn't ask that. "Nothing special, just a date that got canceled."

Vanessa raised an eyebrow. "Anyone I would know?"

"No, he's—" he faltered. Was this the moment to tell his mother about the man he was falling for who wasn't a wolf? "He's a Norm."

Vanessa's eyes widened briefly before she schooled her face back to neutral. "Mixed relationships don't often work out."

Roman looked up sharply and forced down the urge to growl. "I'm aware of the restrictions. I haven't told him anything I shouldn't, and if it gets serious, I'll go through the appropriate channels to get approval before I do tell him."

Vanessa leaned forward, opening her mouth as though to say something, when there was a knock at the door, and Meg stuck her head back into the office.

"Your twelve o'clock is waiting for you in the meeting room, when you're ready." Meg's tone was much more formal this time, and she bobbed her head again before leaving.

"Will you join me?" Vanessa asked.

"If you think that will be welcome. I don't know if they'll want a man they don't know in the room."

"Some strength in numbers will help to demonstrate we're serious, and have the resources to keep them safe, and it would have only been me otherwise. But we'll play it by ear if she responds poorly."

Roman nodded, noting that his mother seemed almost nervous, a state that wasn't natural to her at all. He hadn't had much to do with other shifters; while obviously similar in many ways, there were some tensions between the different shifter clans.

The meeting room led off from the main room at the front of the building. The knitting circle had all left now, only Meg was still there sitting at the desk that served as the reception for greeting people coming into the center. She volunteered at the front desk a day or two every week, making sure people coming in were in the right place. Vanessa nodded to Meg as they passed, as did Roman.

Inside the meeting room were a handful of tables pushed together in the middle, a whiteboard on one side, along with some cupboards and a coffee station, though there weren't any of the sometimes-questionable donuts on offer today. Instead, a selection of sandwiches had been placed in the center of the tables, along with plates and napkins. On the far side sat a woman in her early thirties, and three kids, aged between five and twelve years old, if Roman had to guess, all of whom resembled her strongly. They were huddled together, as though trying to take up the least space they could. It pulled at his guts to see them so clearly terrified, but the woman was trying to put a brave face on it.

"Julie? I'm Vanessa, I'm the Director of the Lupin Center, this is my son, Roman." She approached slowly and didn't attempt to shake the woman's hand. Julie took a half-step backwards, and the children, who were behind her, had to follow suit.

"N-nice to meet you," Julie said, managing to keep the uneasiness out of her voice for the most part. Roman remained silent, nodding his head in her direction, waiting behind his mother and trying to look non-threatening.

"Won't you have a seat? We've arranged for some lunch, so we can get to know one another a bit, and I can explain the way the Center can help you. Does that sound okay?"

Julie nodded, and the three children looked longingly at the food. She whispered to them in a low voice and motioned them forward. The kids took the seats closest to the food and took to it as though they hadn't had steady meals. Roman's heart broke a little more to see the wariness in the woman's stance, and the fear in the children's expressions as he came into the room. The fact people existed who thought it was okay, or somehow justified, to terrorize their families made his hackles rise, and he reminded himself not to let it show, lest they think he was angry at them.

Vanessa sat, taking a plate and a couple of point sandwiches, and motioned to him to sit on her left. Julie had taken some food and was seated with the children on the far side of the table. Her initial fear seemed to be subsiding, but she was still on edge.

"I heard a little bit about your situation from Professor Black, but I would appreciate you telling me about how you ended up… here," Vanessa said, her voice unusually subdued.

Julie swallowed and flicked her eyes over the kids and Roman before beginning. "I'm sure you've heard it all before—the relationship was fiery at the start, which was very romantic, he wanted to be with me all the time, wanted to know where I was, and it seemed sweet, but after we were married, only six months after we met, I know it was very quick, he started to be…" she looked away briefly, "meaner. What was cute and protective at first became possessive and controlling. He didn't like me going out, didn't like me seeing my family."

Vanessa nodded, and Roman listened, using all his concentration to keep his face neutral.

"Each time I got pregnant, he was worse, barely wanted me to leave the house, even for things like groceries, which was hard, especially because all my friends were sick of me canceling plans, and not getting back to them. Anyway, with the youngest, Scott Junior, my husband insisted I had to give up work to be a stay-at-home mom, and then—" she broke off.

"It's tough to tell a stranger these things, I know. You don't have to tell us anything else," Vanessa said, nodding to the children. "What brought you to seek help today?"

"Once I gave up work, I didn't have much connection outside the household, and well, eventually I realized Scott would never be the man I knew before we married. He had changed, and I wouldn't be," she lowered her voice, "safe, until we were living somewhere else." Julie took a bite of her sandwich and chewed it. Roman was worried the children would be put off by the adult conversation, but they were engrossed in the food, it seemed.

"I spoke to my mom in secret, and made some arrangements to leave, but I don't have any money, so getting a rental deposit together and all that stuff was out of my reach. Mom reached out to the Elite, she grew up here, to see if there was anyone who knew of a place we could go while I get back on my feet, someone Scott wouldn't be able to intimidate… and that's how I ended up here."

Vanessa sat back in her chair and clasped her hands. "Interesting that you believe Scott would intimidate anyone who helped you—"

"He would. His family's connected, and well, panthers can be really touchy if they think you're trying to take something away they regard as theirs."

Roman clenched his teeth and tried to calm his thoughts. He wanted to hurt this Scott for making his family run, and for not being able to control his more animal urges. As a wolf, he had been drilled growing up that he could never allow his emotions, whatever they might be, to overtake him. That he was responsible for any harm he caused, shifted or not, and being stronger than other people meant he needed to prevent violence, not perpetrate it.

"It's okay, Roman, we'll make sure Scott is dealt with in the proper way." Vanessa had turned to him and laid her hand over his, which he realized was gripping the arm of the chair. "My son is new to this line of work, and I'm afraid he's still somewhat naïve to the casual cruelty of some people. But he knows how to keep his temper under control, I assure you."

Julie's eyes widened a little as she saw his hands, then she sighed. "I find it hard to trust people, men in particular. I'm very thankful that you're both willing to help."

"Anything I can do to set things right, I'll do it," Roman said. "As my mother said, this is my first time, and I admit it's quite upsetting to hear how you've been treated. I'm sorry if my emotions frightened you."

"Maybe you could take the kids into the main room and find them some pens and paper or something while Julie and I talk logistics. Do you think that would be okay?"

Julie licked her lips and looked away.

"My colleague Meg, she showed you in, will be out there keeping an eye on them, and we can leave the door open so you can see the kids if that makes you more comfortable."

"Yes, that would be good." Julie looked at him again. "I'm sorry."

"I know it's not personal. If I were in your shoes I wouldn't trust strangers with my kids either." Roman smiled, trying again to seem friendly.

"Have you young ones had enough to eat?" Vanessa said. The kids all looked to their mother, before nodding.

"You can go do some drawing with Roman, I'll be right here, and I'll be able to see you the whole time," Julie said.

The three kids stood silently and followed Roman into the main room, a large multifunction area where the knitting circle had been meeting when he arrived. The kids' corner was all set up, so all he had to do was find some paper and the colored pencils. They were hesitant at first, so Roman stepped back and started talking to Meg, keeping half an eye on them while not being too close.

"They've been through a lot," Meg whispered.

"Mmm."

"I've seen too many of them in my time." She shook her head. The phone on the reception desk started to ring and Meg answered it. Roman sat on one of the mismatched chairs and scrolled through his phone. He couldn't hear what his mother and Julie were saying, nor the snippets of whispered conversation between the children, so he tried to keep his mind occupied with catching up with the world at large.

He struggled to keep his mind off the family and their troubles, but he left them to their conversation for almost an hour, at which point Vanessa came out of the meeting room looking harried.

"Roman," she said in a hushed whisper. "I need to ask you a favor."

"Sure, what is it?"

"I've had a call from the police station. One of the young men who comes in here sometimes, Granger, has been arrested. Can you go down there and sit with him? Make sure he doesn't get himself into any more trouble."

"I—" Roman hesitated. "What do you mean sit with him, I'm not a lawyer."

"I know." Vanessa looked over her shoulder towards Julie who was now sitting with the kids. "You don't have to be a lawyer, just be there for him. Make sure the cops are treating him well."

Roman scratched the stubble on his chin. "I'll do my best."

"Aren't you dating a cop now?"

Roman frowned, not wanting to bring Jason into this. Given the attitude the other officers seemed to have towards him, asking him to step in could leave him in an even more compromised position. "Yeah, but he's a rookie, he won't have any influence."

"Even so, if he can help, I want you to ask."

"Alright." Roman had no intention of doing so, but his mother didn't need to know that.

*

The drug bust was over in minutes; Jason and Riley were there to help with crowd control and keeping an eye on those in custody. Back at the station, they were processing the six men who had been arrested, and the detectives had started questioning the youngest of them, a terrified looking man who couldn't have been much older than Jason.

"Have you ever heard of Growl?" Riley said, as she closed the cell door on their last prisoner.

"Growl? Like the sound an angry dog makes?" he asked.

"No." She smiled. "It's a drug, a street name for something apparently, but I don't know what."

"In that case, no. I have no idea what Growl is. Is that what they were looking for at the house earlier?"

"Yeah. I heard one of the detectives talking about it, and asking one of the prisoners, but I haven't come across it either."

"Bell," Watch Commander Ward bellowed through the holding area.

"Yes, sir?"

"You're needed out front. Someone to see your prisoner." The older man turned and marched out of the room before Jason could ask which prisoner, or who was waiting in the lobby for him.

The front lobby of the San Destino Police Station was furnished with rows of beige molded plastic chairs. Usually, there were half a dozen people waiting there at any given time, to see someone in holding, or meet with an officer or detective to give them a statement. Today there were around fifteen, many in their early twenties, looking anxious and fidgety.

"Ward said there was someone here for me?" Jason asked the officer behind the front desk.

"Roman Eldritch is here to see Granger Porter," she said without looking up.

"Did you say Roman Eldritch?"

"Yes, Bell. He's over there." She pointed to where Roman was seated behind a couple of thin-faced young women. Jason walked out from behind the desk, and approached him, his stomach doing backflips and somersaults as he tried to work out how to handle this collision of his personal and private lives.

"Roman?" Jason put his hand on Roman's elbow. Roman startled and turned to him.

"Jason! I uh, didn't realize you'd be here." He frowned. "No, I mean, I knew you were working, but I came to see someone who was just arrested."

"I know. The Watch Commander sent me over to meet the person here for Granger Porter, which is you, I guess?" Jason's hand had lingered on Roman's elbow, and he dropped it, worried his colleagues would see.

"Yes, my mother, you know I said she helps to run a community center, she got the call when Granger was arrested, and sent me."

"Right. I guess it's just bad luck you got stuck with me," Jason said, feeling color rise in his cheeks.

"Or good luck." Roman winked. "So how does this work?"

"Come with me. We can go into an interview room and I'll bring Granger to talk to you. You're not his lawyer, so someone will need to be in the room with you at all times."

"I understand, thank you."

Jason led Roman back into the station, around to the right, where the community liaison rooms were. Warmer and friendlier than the interview rooms, the community liaison rooms were made available for meetings that didn't need to be recorded, though they had CCTV there was no audio.

"Have a seat," Jason said, gesturing to the gray molded plastic chairs arranged around the wood-laminate table. The two men sat in silence for a moment.

"I'm sorry to drop in unannounced like this," Roman said.

"It's fine. Really. Do you do this often, provide support to people in custody?"

Roman chuckled. "No, this is my first time. A favor for my mother. To be honest, I don't know what help I can provide, but I guess moral support will help."

"I'm sure it will. If you're okay here, I'll go get Granger and you can talk."

Roman licked his lips, as though about to say something.

"Do you have any questions?"

"I was just going to ask if you can be the person to stay with us, you know you mentioned someone needs to be in the room. I don't trust anyone more than you."

"It's not really a rookie thing, but I'll do my best."

Roman nodded and squeezed Jason's hand. He stood up and went back to holding, where he checked the cells for Granger Porter.

"You have a visitor." Jason pulled open the hatch in the scratched Perspex door to address the young man. His ash-blond hair was messy, and his light brown eyes looked troubled. He'd been spoken to briefly, according to the notes, but the detectives had put him back in holding to work on someone else.

"A visitor?" He looked confused.

"Yes. I'm going to cuff you, and then you'll need to come with me."

"You okay there, Bell?" Riley asked, coming up behind him.

"Yeah, I'm taking him to see someone in the community liaison rooms."

"Have you done that before?" she said quietly.

"Not on my own, but the visitor is a friend of mine."

Riley chewed her lip for a moment. "If you need me, call over the radio. I'll put it on channel seven."

"Thanks." Jason smiled. Riley would know it wasn't strictly by the book, but she seemed okay with the arrangement. Perhaps it was a sign of trust in him that she would allow him to watch a prisoner alone.

"Put your hands through the hole," he instructed Granger. Jason cuffed the man's hands in front of him and led him to meet Roman with a gentle grip on his upper arm.

"Who's the visitor?"

"Roman Eldritch."

Granger stopped in his tracks, forcing Jason to stop as well. "Something wrong?"

"I didn't think they'd send an Eldritch. I was expecting someone from the center."

"Roman said they sent him, is there a problem? Do you want to go back to holding?"

"No, no. It's fine." Granger's eyes were wide, but he seemed more awed than afraid.

Roman was sitting in the same chair facing the door as when Jason left him earlier. A frown briefly flickered across his face as Jason guided Granger to the seat opposite.

"Because Roman isn't here as your lawyer, I'm required to stay in the room. Anything you say that directly relates to the past, present, or future commission of a crime I'll be forced to report to my colleagues, but anything else is confidential."

Roman nodded, Granger looked anxious.

"How are you, uh, doing?" Roman said, after several long moments of silence.

"I—thank you for coming."

"What were you arrested for?" Roman asked.

"Possession of a controlled substance, with the intent to distribute. It was part of a big raid on a house in Chapel Hill earlier today," Jason answered.

"I see." Roman was looking at the young man intently. "My mother sent me here to provide support, but I don't know what you need. Do you have a lawyer?"

Granger shook his head.

"What happened? I'm sure you wouldn't be at the center if you were dealing drugs. Vanessa wouldn't allow that."

"I live there; I mean in the house where I was arrested. I don't have anywhere else to go."

Roman sighed. Jason was trying not to listen to the conversation, but it was a small room.

"Okay. Well, we'll get someone from legal aid to help you. In the meantime don't say anything else."

"They were asking me about Growl," Granger's voice had dropped to barely more than a whisper.

"I just told you not to say anything else, didn't I? What did you tell them?"

"Nothing. I don't know anything about it, other than you know the basics everyone knows."

"Good. That's probably not going to hurt you, but I really need to stress that you say nothing at all to anyone until legal aid gets here."

Granger nodded.

"Are you okay for medication or whatever? Do you need me to get anything from your house?"

"No, I don't think so. I'm not taking any medications."

Roman and Granger shared a look that Jason didn't understand, but it seemed they were wrapping the conversation up.

"If you do need anything, call the Center. We'll make sure you're looked after. I'll have a lawyer sent over as soon as we can organize someone."

Granger nodded again and looked at Jason, apprehension still all over his face, but he was sitting a bit taller in his chair and perhaps felt a bit more confident.

"I'll take you back to holding. If you'll wait here, please, Roman, then I'll walk you out."

He was silent on the walk back to the cells, and Granger seemed calmer, though quieter.

"If you want to come with me, we'll head out." Jason popped his head back into the community liaison room to collect Roman. He stood and they walked out through the lobby into the parking lot out the front of the San Destino PD.

"I'm sorry if that was weird," Jason said.

"I'm sorry too. It was… I suppose it would have been weird for me either way. I've never been to a police station to support someone in custody before."

Jason nodded and pushed down the urge to hold Roman's hand for comfort. "Do you know anything about Growl?" he asked, immediately regretting it when Roman's face darkened, and a frown formed between his gorgeous eyebrows.

"What do you mean?"

"Until today, I hadn't come across it. I guess I was wondering if you had any intel, like, at all—the detectives never tell us anything." Jason hoped he seemed nonchalant, but he was desperate to learn about this new drug.

Roman ran a hand over the back of his neck, looking at Jason for a long moment before answering. "I don't know a lot, except I think it's an herb or plant, like marijuana. People get it in little baggies and you can smoke it or eat it cooked into food. I've heard most people don't react to it, but there are some groups that really get a great high from it. Sort of mellow and euphoric. In certain circles it's very sought after, not very addictive, especially if it doesn't have much of an effect on you."

"Interesting. I wonder why some people don't react to it?" Jason said, almost to himself.

"I don't know for sure, but the theory is there are some families, or maybe genetic mutations that are needed for it to get you high—like how birds can eat chili peppers because they don't have the receptor for capsaicin."

"I didn't know that about birds. That's useful, about the Growl I mean."

They were silent for a beat. Jason didn't want the moment to end, but he needed to get back to work, and standing around in the parking lot could easily become awkward, not to mention suspicious if people saw them.

"Well, let me know if Granger needs anything else, you have my number, obviously, otherwise you can contact the Lupin Center, they'll help you, or try to put you in touch with people who can." Roman looked at his watch. "I'd better be going, lots of stuff to do for Mom."

"Yes, sounds like a full-time job. Don't let her push you around though, yeah?"

"I won't. I appreciate the concern." Roman held out his hand for a handshake.

"Any time." Jason shook his hand trying to say, 'I love you' without words. He seemed to appreciate it, giving a final nod before walking across the parking lot and back towards Bloomington.

Chapter 5

As soon as Granger had mentioned Growl, Roman knew he would have to involve his mother in the case. What he couldn't tell Jason, as a Norm, was that the drug had been specifically developed for werewolves and shifters, and had very little effect on Norms, and other sorts of Paranorms.

If that raid was looking for Growl, his mother and the Wolf Council needed to know. Now he thought about it, he wasn't sure how the police would have been tipped off without someone in the Paranorm community, or even the Elite, telling them to raid. He pulled out his phone and called Vanessa.

"Roman, how did you go? Did you see Granger?"

"Hi, Mom. Yeah, I saw him. He seems… confused to say the least. What do you know about Growl?"

"Growl? You mean that drug? Very little. Why?"

"According to Granger that's what they were looking for. I don't see how they would know about it without Elite involvement."

"Well," his mother said, "there are more Paranorms in the police than you might think. But you're right, it's concerning that we weren't notified that there was a raid coming. Usually, we're told about these things in advance."

Roman was silent, thinking over the implications of Granger's arrest, and what they could possibly do to help.

"You saw Granger?" Vanessa prompted.

"Yeah, Jason helped me, and he stayed in the room while we talked, so I couldn't say everything I wanted to. We only had a few minutes together. I don't really know what else I can do, as I said I'm not a lawyer."

"It helps to see a friendly face, to know we're still supporting him, and you're my son, that means something."

Roman made a sound of agreement and chewed on his bottom lip. "What do you want me to do now?"

"Can you stay around the station for a while? See if you can catch Jason and get any information from him about the raid and any charges being laid against Granger. If possible, see if you can find out what evidence they have."

"I'm not sure how successful I'll be at that. They'll probably clam up if I start asking anything like that."

"Maybe, but Jason is a friend, more than a friend. I'm sure you can use that to your advantage. I'll send you the details of a lawyer we have an arrangement with who can come down and look into it."

"Yeah, okay." Roman looked around the parking lot and back towards the air-conditioned station. It was sweltering under the late summer sun. "I'll check in if I get any more info."

As he stepped back towards the lobby, he saw Jason heading back out.

"Hey, I'm glad you're still here," he said.

"I'm gonna stick around for a while, in case Granger needs anything else, and to call his lawyer."

"That's good." Jason darted his eyes around, as though scanning for people who might overhear. They had moved into the shade, but the heat radiating off the blacktop was still causing sweat to run down inside his shirt—wolves tended to run hot, and summer was not their ideal climate.

"Is there something I should know?"

"I shouldn't say anything…" Jason said.

"Okay." The silence hung in the air between them. Roman's mind kept returning to the gloriously cool lobby just out of his reach.

"If someone is arrested as part of a raid, especially a drugs bust, the police usually have to have some evidence that they're involved further than just being in the area. I didn't get the impression Granger had anything illegal in his possession. I guess I'm worried he's got caught up in something just by being in the house, and I wanted to make sure he had support, y'know, legally."

"The Center has a contact, I'm about to make a call about that."

"I wouldn't want to speak ill of my colleagues, but sometimes they can be a bit over enthusiastic. It would be good if his lawyer knew that there was no possession, at least as far as I could see."

"That's great to know. I'll pass that on. I…" Roman paused, considering the wisdom of saying any more. "I was wondering if you know where the tip came from?"

Jason frowned and rubbed his hand absently across his mouth. "I don't know. I'm worried that there's a drug out there that I know nothing about. Well, almost nothing."

"As I said before, it's not hard stuff—I didn't even know it was illegal until today, not that I've tried it, but I know some people who have."

"I'll keep asking around though. I should be aware of any substance that might be misused in the community."

"Yeah, I guess it might help." Roman tried to make his tone light but wasn't sure it worked. Jason seemed to relax a little, as though having divulged that there wasn't much evidence against Granger, a weight had been lifted from his shoulders. They both headed back to the lobby, and Jason went back to work.

Roman sat on the plastic chairs for another hour or two. After calling the lawyer and getting confirmation that they would send someone, he stared into space or scrolled on his phone.

If he told Jason about werewolves and shifters, about his true self, then he could explain why Growl worked for some people and not others. If he was honest with himself, he also wanted to have the conversation sooner rather than later because if Jason freaked out and broke up with him, it was better to get it over with. He couldn't stand the idea of not having him in his life, but it would hurt less now than in six months. At least he hoped that was true.

When five o'clock rolled around, Roman started to think the lawyer wasn't coming. He called their office and left a voicemail, but he wasn't optimistic.

He texted Jason:

> *Are you still at work?*

While he waited for a reply, he sent an update to his mom.

> *Granger is still in holding, I told him to wait for the legal counsel, but when I called the firm, they said they would send someone, and they haven't arrived yet. Do I keep waiting? Did you get Julie and her kids set up somewhere?*

He tapped his phone on the palm of his left hand, frustrated at having spent all afternoon staring into space in the lobby of the police station—it wasn't that it felt like a waste of time exactly, but he felt helpless, something Roman hated feeling.

He stood up and paced up and down; the crowd had thinned out and only three others were waiting now. The middle-aged female officer behind the desk stared at him disapprovingly, and he sat down again.

> *Probably a lost cause today. You may as well head home. We'll send someone else tomorrow, along with getting legal aid sorted out. Thanks for being there. Julie's all set up. xx Mom.*

Vanessa had a habit of signing her texts, even though no one else in the world did. Roman shook his head at his mother's disinclination towards technology.

"Roman?" Jason's voice broke into his thoughts.

"Hey."

"I didn't think you'd still be here." Jason was in his civilian clothes again. "I've just finished my shift."

"Yeah, I've been sitting here like a lemon all day trying to get legal aid to come down and feeling totally useless."

"Legal aid can take a long time, but Granger has asked for his lawyer and the detectives won't be able to question him until someone shows up—likely tomorrow now."

"That's what my mom said. I was about to head out." Roman thought about the aborted plans they'd had for the day, and how he wished he could go home and eat take-out with Jason, but he also felt a frisson of tension between them, as though the unspoken part of his life was more obvious now.

"Do you want to… uh…" Jason started.

"Hang out?"

"Yeah, I dunno, have a drink or something?"

"That sounds good." Roman longed to take Jason into his arms and kiss him until he forgot about Growl and anything he might have picked up about the paranormal world, but he knew that would only be a temporary solution. They left the station in silence. Walking beside his lover while maintaining a platonic aloofness was more of a burden than he'd anticipated.

"Can I give you a ride?" Jason said, pointing to his car in the lot.

"Sure."

The car ride was similarly subdued. Roman wasn't sure how to open the conversation. Jason was deep in thought too, it seemed, though about what he couldn't speculate.

They pulled up to the curb in front of Roman's sharehouse a little while later.

"Do you want to come in? My roommates might be inside, but you're welcome."

"I don't know if I'm feeling very sociable. Would we need to hang out with them?" Jason rubbed his two forefingers along either side of the bridge of his nose.

"No, we can grab beers and hang out in my room if you want."

Jason nodded and turned off the engine.

Roman's roommates weren't home, perhaps they'd gone out for food or to a bar, and they sat in the kitchen with a couple of beers.

"Is there something on your mind?" Roman asked, after a heavy few minutes of silence.

"I'm sorry. I should go."

"That's not what I meant. You're so chatty normally, and now you're quieter than I've ever seen you. I'm concerned. Did something happen on your shift?"

"No… well, yes. I got called in for a big drug bust, and we didn't find anything except this Growl, which people have been giving me mixed messages about all day, and I don't know what's going on. I feel like there's something everyone knows but me, and I hate it."

Roman ran his hand over his stubble in thought. It was a perfect opportunity to start a conversation about things in San Destino that were not exactly normal, but it was forbidden to tell a Norm without permission from the elders.

"That sounds unpleasant. Can I help?"

"Am I crazy? Or is there something going on?"

"You're not crazy," Roman said quietly.

"So, tell me, why does a drug I've just learned about today only work on some people? And why are we doing a raid for something that isn't even illegal, according to the California Penal Code? And why won't anyone give me a straight answer?"

"Who's not giving you a straight answer? Who have you talked to about this?"

Jason waved his hand dismissively. "I mentioned it to Riley, she's my TO sometimes, and she was very vague, mentioned something about a special San Destino subsection, but I couldn't find it anywhere, and then the detectives in charge of the raid both brushed off my questions. Granted, the detectives are probably busy processing everyone and writing up their reports, but it felt like I was being gaslit or something, y'know?"

Roman nodded. He wanted to explain, but he hadn't sought the permission, and he wasn't sure how Jason would react.

"I'm really hoping you can tell me something that will make it all make sense." Jason had started peeling the label off his beer in frustration.

"I'm trying to figure out where to start." Roman was stalling, he knew it, but it was so delicate. "Have you ever seen things in San Destino that you couldn't explain?"

Jason looked up sharply, his brows furrowed. "What?"

"Have you had a situation where weird things happened, and the world just shouldn't work like that?"

Jason's frown deepened and he looked back at the beer bottle. "There was one time. At a vehicle collision, the EMT was working on someone, and I was sure they were dead, but then the EMT put his hand on the person, took off his glove and everything, which was weird in itself, and then they were breathing again. I guess they must not have been dead, but they really looked it."

"Okay. Anything else?"

"Not really. I guess we do get a lot more animal attacks in the city than I would have thought was normal. I didn't realize until I started on patrol, but there are some feral animals out there."

Roman nodded again. He would have to ask forgiveness instead of permission. He hoped that his mother would understand, and that, for once, being her son would help him, instead of making him a target for bullies and unrealistic expectations.

"I want to tell you something, but I need you to understand that you can't tell anyone else. I mean no one. Can I trust you with keeping my confidence?"

Jason widened his eyes as though hurt. "You don't have much faith in me if you think I can't keep a secret."

"I'm not just talking about me here. This could hurt a lot of people, and it's not just my secret. I need you to give me your word you won't say anything."

"I'll keep what you tell me in confidence, but you know if you're disclosing a crime, or an imminent risk to someone's safety, I have to report it."

"I promise it's neither of those things, so I agree to the exception." Roman took a deep breath in and sighed heavily. This could go sideways very quickly. Even if Jason believed what he was about to tell him, he'd kept a fundamental part of himself from him.

"San Destino is not like other places. There are things that happen here, people who live here, who are not what you might call normal." Roman looked up to check Jason's expression, but it was unreadable. "The EMT you saw may have been a witch—"

"You can't be serious," Jason interrupted.

"It sounds ridiculous, but there's magic in San Destino. It's a place of congruence for a lot of things, and both the place and the people have unusual powers."

"So, bringing someone back from the dead, that's a real thing, is it?"

"They might not have been truly dead, but I believe that EMT was using healing powers beyond the usual medical supplies."

Jason pressed his lips together and looked skeptical.

"And all the maulings, there's a reason for a lot of those, and it's not animal attacks… it's shapeshifters."

"No way. There's no way shapeshifters are real."

"I don't mean the sort that can be any shape. I mean wolf shifters, panther shifters, I think there are some bear shifters. They have one human form, and one animal form, and they can go between them at will."

"That's not any better. If you don't want to tell me what's really going on, just say so and I'll go home. I don't need fairy stories."

Roman sighed. "I can show you, but I don't want to frighten you."

"Show me what exactly?"

"I uh…" Roman hesitated. "I'm one of them; I'm a wolf shifter."

Jason stared for a moment, blinking rapidly. "No, you're not."

"I am. I'm sorry I didn't say anything, but we're sworn to secrecy. The Wolf Council, that my mother is the leader of, along with the Council of Elite who help to run the city, have rules about who can know about the paranormal population."

"You're making this up. I've never heard about any of that."

"You're a Norm, of course you wouldn't. It would be a breach of the secrecy agreement for you to know, and if you did come across something that was too obvious to ignore, there are people whose job it is to work little memory charms and stop you remembering."

Jason started to look frightened. "You've really lost the plot, haven't you?"

"I promise I haven't. I'll show you the wolf, but I want you to remember it's still me, I'm not a threat to you, and you're safe." Roman rubbed his hands along his jeans, trying to dispel some of the anxiety. "And you're not mad, it's real."

"No, I don't think I want that. I think I should… uh, go."

"Remember how Growl only works on some people? How you were trying to make sense of it? Well, the reason is, it only works for shifters and werewolves. Like catnip, it's derived from an herb that affects shifters, and not regular humans."

Jason had been leaning away, as though trying to distance himself from the apparently crazy person in front of him, but now started to lean forward. "A drug that only works on shifters? I suppose if there were such a thing as shifters, it would make sense that they were sensitive to different substances."

"I know you don't believe me. The best way for me to show you this is real is to shift to my wolf self. It's a bit scary, I'm quite a big, dark gray wolf, but I promise, you're safe."

At this, Jason's eyes widened again, this time in fear. Having started the conversation, Roman knew he needed to make him believe, otherwise he might go around telling people his boyfriend was crazy. "Are you ready?"

"No. It's okay. I believe you."

"You don't; you think I'm nuts. I would think I was nuts in your shoes. I'll shift straight back, okay, just a few seconds as the wolf and then back to me. Okay?"

Before Jason could say anything else, Roman stood up and backed up into a more open part of the kitchen. His wolf self took up quite a different space to his human self. The shift took a couple of seconds, and while it didn't exactly hurt, it was very uncomfortable, like stretching out a tight muscle, but all over your body all at once. He squared his shoulders, then got down on his hands and knees on the kitchen floor, allowing the shift to wash over him.

He looked up through his wolf eyes at Jason who was now standing and backing away, face full of panic. The shift back was slightly less uncomfortable but still required concentration. Once he was back in his human form on the kitchen floor he stood, and walked towards Jason, who was looking pale and unwell.

"It's just me. You're okay," he said in a calm, soothing voice. Jason shook his head mutely. "Come back and sit on the chair. I don't want you fainting."

Jason allowed himself to be led back to the chair and sat heavily. For a few long minutes, neither of them spoke. Roman was holding one of Jason's hands, idly rubbing his thumb over the skin on the back of his hand. After a few minutes Jason flinched away, withdrawing his hand.

"What the fuck?"

"It's a lot to take in."

"I was sure you were crazy. You were delusional and somehow I hadn't noticed. Maybe you were on a psychotic break, but now I think I might be crazy."

"You're not. San Destino is a weird place, a haven for paranormal types, but you couldn't have known. Unless you're specifically brought in, like I've just done."

"How many of you are there?"

"What, wolf shifters?"

"To start with, yes."

"A couple of hundred. My family, and my housemates are all shifters. We have a pretty tight-knit community. That's why Mom is so involved in the Lupin Center. She's looking out for the wolf shifter community, making sure people have what they need, and don't do things like kill people while they're in their wolf form."

"How many people with uh… powers or whatever are there in San Destino?" Jason's face was very pale, and he was breathing fast and shallow.

"Deep breaths, remember?"

"How many in San Destino?" Jason repeated.

"I don't know, but I would guess half. Maybe more."

Jason's eyes were wild. "And you've all been lying about it? You lied to me our whole relationship! When were you going to tell me?"

"You have to understand—"

"I don't have to understand anything, you're a liar." Jason's fear was being replaced by anger, something easier to process, but just as volatile.

"I was going to tell you when the time was right, before you met my family." He reached out again; he wanted more than anything to comfort Jason, to hold him and tell him it would be alright, that no matter how much it felt like his world was crumbling around him, the world hadn't changed, only his point of view, but Jason wouldn't have it.

"I can't be with someone who lies like it's as natural as talking. I'm leaving. Don't contact me. I never want to see you again."

Roman let his hand drop and watched the man he loved run from him. He stood in the kitchen after the front door slammed for a long time, before sitting down with a deep sigh. Of all the ways he thought that conversation might have gone, he never expected it to be so catastrophically bad.

Chapter 6

Jason ran from the house, fighting the tears that threatened to come. When he'd woken up that morning in Roman's bed, he had been imagining a life with him, but now everything was falling apart. His whole view of the world had to change along with it, all he thought he knew about his boyfriend—ex-boyfriend now he supposed—was wrong. He drove towards his home in Hazelwood not really thinking about what he was doing, just wanting to be away from the terrifying wolf that had stood in Roman's kitchen only minutes before.

As his panic ebbed away, he slowed down and looked around him. He was walking close to Starfall Beach, and he wondered if the calm lapping of the waves might help him think. The night was balmy, but the breeze off the water was cool, and he shivered as the sweat he'd worked up evaporated. Jason got out of the car, sat on a large rock, and looked out over the water—it was flat and still, the tiny ripples reflecting the stars and waxing gibbous moon.

He thought about all the times he'd come across stuff that didn't make sense in his job, and in his life. The EMT who appeared to bring someone back to life, the bodies he'd had to stand guard over that looked as though they'd been torn apart by wild animals, the flashes he'd seen out of the corner of his eye that didn't make sense, but when he looked over, they were always gone. The more he thought about it, the more he understood he'd been surrounded by paranormal stuff his whole life and not known it.

Would it have been better not to know? To have nothing to bring to mind when he thought about the strange goings on in San Destino? Maybe. It would mean Roman was losing it, but he couldn't dismiss what he'd said, there were just too many things that confirmed what he'd said.

And of course, he'd turned into a fucking wolf right there in the kitchen; that was a sight he would never forget. If what he said was true, half the population of San Destino were somehow supernatural, it boggled the mind. But at the same time, it made sense.

Jason wondered how many of his police colleagues knew about it—or how many cops were paranormal. He would probably never know, since they weren't allowed to tell anyone, and if he asked another regular person, they'd think he was nuts. He looked down at his hands, which he had been idly twisting together and sighed.

The world as I know it has changed, he thought. And then there was Roman, a man he thought he loved, who had hidden a huge part of his identity from him. Yes, he had a good reason, but it was still a betrayal. Not to mention the question of whether Jason was okay with dating someone who could turn into a wolf at any moment and rip his throat out. If they ever fought, if Roman turned out to be an abusive asshole, he could be dead in moments, and Roman would get away with it.

Jason shuddered. His butt was cold against the rock, and the light breeze from earlier was now too cold for comfort. He stood, got back in the car, and made his way back home. When he got there, the front porch light was on, and Holly was sitting on the sofa watching some sort of fashion competition reality show.

"You're home late. I thought you would have stayed with Roman if you weren't home by now."

Jason shook his head slowly; he couldn't form words. Holly paused her show and looked at him in the ghostly light cast from the TV.

"Wait, what happened? Did you break up? Is that what this is?"

Jason nodded, and a hot tear rolled down his cheek. Holly jumped up from the couch and rushed over to wrap him in her arms.

"What did that bastard do? I'll kill him. I thought you'd found the one, he seemed so good for you." She was babbling, but her hug and her hand stroking his hair felt nice even while his heart was breaking.

"He… didn't tell me something big and now I can't trust him. So, I told him I never wanted to see him again," Jason mumbled into her T-shirt.

"What was it?"

"I…" Jason hesitated. "I can't say, it's personal, but it's something you would tell your boyfriend, and he didn't. I don't know if he was ever going to tell me except that—" Jason struggled to explain the revelation without divulging to Holly all the paranormal stuff in San Destino. He swallowed and went on, "Except that he came into the station today to support someone and it all came out later this evening. Anyway, I can't trust him anymore and… yeah." Jason was exhausted. All the drama of the raid, seeing Roman in the station, all the stuff he had to process about the world along with his anger at Roman had left him feeling drained and boneless.

"I'm sorry, honey. I know you liked him." Holly released her hug and took his hand. "Come watch the rest of this episode with me. You don't have to talk, just hang here, and then when you're ready, crawl into bed."

Jason nodded and let himself be pulled towards the big squishy couch. He didn't follow the show, but it didn't matter, his mind wouldn't have focused even if he did. His eyelids felt heavy, and gritty with unshed tears, but he would cry later. For now, he would sit here with his best friend and try to deal with all the things that had changed since that morning.

*

Roman stayed in his kitchen for a long while, disbelieving that his coming out had gone so spectacularly badly. He had expected it to be a shock, and he'd expected the accusation of lying, but he'd hoped Jason might understand the necessity of it all.

He shook his head. It was a betrayal, having to hide something so big about himself, but it still felt like rejection. Maybe this was why his mother went on and on about dating within the community.

While he was sitting there trying to make sense of it all, his roommates came home, the three of them chatty and jovial until they saw his face.

"What happened to you? You look like someone killed your pet," Austin said, the youngest of his roommates and the one with the least effective filter between brain and mouth.

"Shut up, Austin." Brad smacked Austin in the shoulder playfully. "Seriously though, you look like crap. Are you okay, bro?"

When they spoke to him the spell was broken, and Roman sighed. "I told Jason about… y'know, being a wolf."

"Oh shit," Toby said, his voice hushed. They were all quiet. Every one of them had had the experience of revealing their true selves to someone, whether a friend or a lover, and had all had it go sideways on them. They knew his pain, not that it made it any less intense in that moment.

"He took it badly then?" Brad asked.

Roman nodded. "Said he never wants to see me again."

"That's rough, dude, I'm sorry. He seemed like a keeper that one." Toby put a hand on his shoulder.

"He's a Norm right? I'd say give him a couple of days, then apologize. See if he comes 'round after getting used to the idea of paranormal forces," Brad said.

Roman looked up. "Has that ever worked for you?"

"Well, I've never dated a Norm."

"Did you get permission to tell him? I thought we weren't supposed to, like, give out that info," Austin said, and again Brad smacked him in the shoulder.

"I didn't. I'm going to have to go to my mom and beg forgiveness for that too… although Jason was mixed up in a Growl case, so I don't know how long he was going to stay ignorant for if I hadn't told him."

"Since when did the cops get involved with Growl?" Toby asked.

"I had the same question, not that I could ask Jason without, you know, telling him everything. They raided a place in Chapel Hill earlier today, lots of arrests, Mom called me in to play support for one of her Lupin Center clients."

"So, your whole day has been one disaster after another?" Toby said.

"You could say that."

"Beer time. I'll get the grill going. We'll drown your sorrows, and tomorrow we can start on a plan to get Jason back."

The last thing Roman wanted to do was drink with his roommates, but he also knew that pulling the lone wolf act was the worst thing he could do for his mental health at the best of times, and now that he'd had his identity thrown back in his face, being around his fellow wolves would probably be good for him. Tomorrow he would be back at work in the afternoon, giving him time to suck up to his mother in the morning. He ran his hand across his face and tried not to think about how his plans for a future with Jason had all come crumbling down.

A Wolf of His Own

The next morning, Roman woke a little after nine feeling seedy. His mouth was furry and dry, and he remembered he hadn't brushed his teeth after several beers and a burned burger or two. He took a deep breath and nearly sobbed at the whiff of Jason's scent still lingering on the bedclothes.

I'll have to change the sheets if I want to get away from that, he thought. On the other hand, maybe it was a nice reminder of what he was working to get back. He needed to be at the bar by four, and he would have time to go by the Lupin Center, even if it took him a while to get out of bed, showered, and down there.

"Two visits in as many days, Roman, that's gotta be a new record," Meg said, beaming at him as he entered the center a little before midday.

"Hey, yeah, I'm looking for my mom."

"She's in her office, hun. Go on through."

Roman ducked his head in thanks and walked back through the narrow corridors to the office where his mother could be found.

He knocked on the open door and stuck his head in. "Have you got a minute?"

Vanessa looked up, frowning, then her face softened into a smile. "Roman, I wasn't expecting you again today, was I?"

"No."

"I always have a minute for you, though it might not be much more than that; I'm still swamped after that damned police raid yesterday."

Roman mumbled agreement, then closed the office door and took a seat in one of the chairs in front of his mother's desk.

"Are you alright? You look worried." Vanessa said, closing her laptop and looking deep into his eyes. "Is it boy trouble?"

"In a way. I don't want you to get angry, but—"

"That is the worst way to start a sentence, son."

"If you'd let me finish," Roman clenched his jaw briefly, trying not to let his frustration show. "I did see Jason at work yesterday, he was supervising Granger for part of his shift, as I told you. At the end of his shift, he came to find me and wanted to talk about Growl; what it was, why he hadn't heard about it."

"And what did you tell him?"

Roman paused. "This is where you might be angry… I told him everything. Well, not everything, but I told him about the wolves, and some of the other paranormal residents here in town." He put up his hand as though to stop her objection. "I know that I didn't have permission from the Council to do that. I am fully prepared to take whatever punishment the Council deems fit, but I really felt Jason was on the cusp of discovering something that a memory charm wouldn't easily erase, and I made the executive decision to tell him, so he didn't find it out in half-truths and rumors."

Vanessa leaned back in her chair, her face like thunder, but she was quiet. If she'd started yelling, he would have understood, he'd expected that, but this silent reaction was unnerving.

"I don't approve of your telling people without the Council's permission; however, your reasoning was sound. If you were to get serious with Jason, which is the direction I suspected you were headed, you would have had to bring him into the know at some point, and his involvement, the police's involvement, in this Growl bust is very troubling indeed. Does he know any more about where they got the tip from? Or what's going to happen to those they've arrested?"

"I might have blown that too. He didn't exactly take the news well, and said, and I quote, 'I never want to see you again.'"

"I see." Vanessa stood up, walked around her desk to perch on the front. She took Roman's hand in hers in an uncharacteristically tender gesture. "I'm sorry it went that way."

"Me too." Roman pushed down the tears he felt building in his throat.

"He might come around. Give him a few days to adjust and reach out again."

Roman gave a hollow laugh. "Brad said the same thing."

"I've always said he was the wisest of the fools you live with."

"Mom!" Roman objected.

"I'm sure they'll grow into responsible members of the community at some point, but at the moment they're stupid, young, and impulsive. Not their fault entirely, but I do wonder if they'll get themselves into trouble sometime and I'll have to step in."

"So, you're not mad about me telling Jason?"

Vanessa shook her head slowly. "It was inevitable really. I just hope he's sensible enough to keep the information to himself. We really don't know who he can trust. I'd always assumed there were a few Paranorms in the San Destino Police force, but by and large I expected they were unaware of the other part of the population. Now they're raiding Growl though, we'll have to tighten our security and put the word around the networks that the cops are arresting people for using."

"You're really not angry?"

"No, after yesterday, and your recent interest in the Center, I trust your judgement here. It would have been easier to justify to the rest of the Council if you'd asked for permission first, but I suppose we can use the raids to argue it was urgent."

Roman nodded. The idea he had of his mother as a hot-blooded woman with a temper may have been wrong, or perhaps she didn't share this more measured version of herself with her children. The angry mom character worked well to keep her kids in line, except they were both older now, and maybe she could chill out a bit.

"Once he's had time to get used to everything, you should try to get some more out of him about the Growl raids. I'm much more worried about the possible effects of that on our community than you telling your boyfriend about us."

Roman shifted in his seat. "I don't know if we can still call him my boyfriend, he was adamant he didn't want to see me."

"In that moment, yes, I'm sure that was true. But let's give him a chance to change his mind. Maybe if you grovel a bit it might help."

"This just got too weird. I think I should go before you start asking about our sex life."

"I didn't realize you were such a prude," Vanessa said, her small smile showing she was teasing him, but he was definitely not comfortable enough to keep talking about it with her.

"I'm leaving that little prod right alone. I'll see myself out, but call me if there's any development with Granger, won't you?"

Vanessa nodded. "I will."

*

Jason had been so angry when he left Roman's place the night before, but he woke up feeling depleted. Sadness that felt bone deep, and hurt at having been lied to. Not only that, but betrayed that someone he had shared a bed with so many times would hide something so fundamental. It made Jason question whether he really knew him at all.

He wasn't working that day, and he hadn't made any plans, having developed a habit of keeping his time free in case Roman had wanted to get together. He lay in bed staring up for a long time after he woke up, trying to psych himself up to get up and face the first day without Roman in his life, but in the end it was his bladder that made the decision for him.

Once out of bed, it was easier to convince himself to go to the kitchen for coffee and breakfast. Holly was at work, their rosters almost never matched up, which made it hard to spend time together. He didn't have many friends, and those he did have weren't the type to discuss the possibility that San Destino was full of magical weirdos and shapeshifters. Jason made himself oatmeal, which he ate without really tasting it, and he burned the coffee.

In his mind, he trawled through everyone he knew trying to figure out if they might be secretly paranormal, and he came up empty until he remembered a conversation with Riley about things they couldn't explain. She seemed to know something, but how much was the question. It could be that she didn't know any more than him, but on the other hand she could have been protecting the secret code and not divulging details to someone who didn't already know. He texted Riley:

> *Hey, are you on shift today? I wanted to ask your advice on something kinda delicate.*

Riley replied a few minutes later.

> *I'm on late tonight, starting at seven, so I have a bit of time now. Should I call you?*

> *No, let's meet up, meet you in Juniper Hollow in an hour?*

Riley replied with her agreement, and he swallowed the last mouthful of crappy coffee before heading to the shower.

As Jason approached Zia Milla's, Riley was saying goodbye to Petra, her girlfriend. He'd met her once after a shift, and he would have recognized her huge pile of curly red hair anywhere.

"Hey," he said, pulling up a chair next to Riley, who was sitting at one of the tables on the sidewalk. "Petra not staying?"

"Nah, she has a class in half an hour, she just walked down with me." Riley smiled. Petra was a yoga teacher as well as providing palliative care for people in the aged care facility in town.

"Cool." Jason wasn't sure exactly how to broach the conversation. How do you bring something like what Roman said up?

"How's that boy of yours doing? You have a face on that says not so good."

"Funny you should ask… that's sort of what I wanted to talk to you about."

"Okay." Riley let the words hang there, and Jason wished he'd thought this through more on the way here. While he was thinking, they were saved by a waitress who came to take their orders.

"Take your time. I'm here for you," Riley said, her eyes sad.

"It's hard to know where to start." Jason stared at his shoes, white sneakers which had become sort of gray after he went camping one time.

"So, you know that raid yesterday?"

"Yeah."

"Roman knows a bit about Growl. He was telling me about how it only affects some people."

"I've heard that." Riley sipped the coffee that had since been delivered to their table.

"He said he could explain why, but that it would reveal something about him that I might not like—"

"Don't tell me he's a user. I have a lot of empathy for substance abuse issues, but I wouldn't ever date someone who uses."

"It wasn't that. He umm…" Jason looked up. Riley was staring at him intently, her manner was kind, but he didn't know how much she already knew. "Do you remember that time we were on patrol out by the pier? And we had a conversation about the weird stuff that happens here sometimes?"

Riley frowned. "Vaguely."

"How much do you know about the strange goings on in San Destino?"

"A little. What does this have to do with it?"

Jason sipped his coffee, stalling for time. "I am going to tell you what Roman told me, but you have to promise not to say anything to anyone."

"You know I will keep any secret that doesn't involve the commission of a crime, or risk of harm to a person."

"Thank you. Well, Roman is… he's a wolf shifter."

Riley's eyes widened for a moment. "A wolf shifter?"

"Yeah, do you, um, know what that is?"

"I do. I'm surprised you do, though I guess it makes sense that at some point if you're dating a Paranorm they have to tell you."

"You don't think I'm crazy? Or that Roman is crazy?"

"No, I have some small abilities, nothing to compare with the witches or shifters of the world, but enough to know a little bit about the secret world that lives in San Destino. Petra is more involved than I am, but even so we're both only on the fringes."

Jason's mind was spinning. It was one thing to have Roman tell him these things, to turn into a wolf right there in front of him, but for Riley, one of the most grounded, sensible people he'd known, to take it in her stride with barely more than a blink suddenly made it all too real.

"It's a lot to take in. Most of the force don't know anything about it, and obviously there's a lot of good reasons to keep these sorts of things under wraps."

"That's what Roman said, but why? Wouldn't it be better for everyone if everything was out in the open?"

Riley licked her lips before she answered. "It might seem like that, but let's go through it logically. When you learned about the paranormal world, what was your first thought?"

"I was frightened. I thought Roman was going to hurt me."

"Right. People are afraid of what they don't understand. Put that together with superhuman strength, magic, and all the rest, people are going to be terrified of their neighbors. All it would take is one person to be a bit too trigger happy and we'd have the start of a panic. Innocent people would be hurt, or possibly killed, and then the Paranorm and Norm communities alike would be out for revenge. It would be chaos."

"What if you just told a couple of people to start, and then a few more, not like a news broadcast or whatever?"

"You'd have the same issue—they'd tell their friends, the friends would tell their friends, and before you know it, the community grapevine has spread the word just as effectively."

"But Roman told me?"

"He did, and think about what that cost him? He's probably worried you'll break up with him, or worse, get a posse together and kill him for what he is."

"I would never hurt him."

"I know that, but put yourself in his shoes—he can't know how you'll take it. That's why he didn't tell you."

Jason mulled over the idea. He'd seen riots and other large crowds and they were unpredictable and often violent. Add to that fear of the unknown and it was a recipe for something terrible. It still hurt that Roman couldn't trust him with his true self, but he was starting to see that he had to protect himself.

"I said I never wanted to see him again."

"That's rather final. Do you still feel that way?"

"I don't know," Jason said. "I'm still angry, but I'm starting to understand why he did it."

"It stings, but you could also look at it that he trusts you now, enough to tell you the biggest, scariest secret he has."

Jason looked at Riley, trying to work out if she was teasing him.

"I'm serious. It's a big risk he took. You could tell people his secret, you could hold it against him, try to take advantage of him… or more likely, react so badly he loses you."

"That seems a bit far-fetched."

"Does it? Is there anything you haven't told him?"

Jason shifted in his seat, considering all the things he and Roman had talked about, and all the things he hadn't said. "I guess there are some things I haven't been completely honest about, but they're little things. Not big things like the fact I can—" he dropped his voice to a whisper, "turn into a wolf whenever I want."

"You have the right to be upset. It's a lot to take in, and you'll have to work out for yourself whether you can date him now he's revealed himself. But don't be too hasty. Give it some time to mull over in your mind. Maybe you can catch up with him in a couple of days and talk it out rather than just throwing your hands in the air and saying it's over."

"Hey! You make me sound like I had some sort of toddler tantrum."

Riley raised one eyebrow and took her time to reply. "Your feelings are valid, no matter what they are, but you also need to reflect. All I'm saying is really think about whether you're willing to give up your relationship for this."

"Alright." He didn't have to like it, but it was probably good advice. "So, what's been happening with you and Petra?" He turned the conversation to more general topics, having hashed out all he wanted to about Roman. It was something that he would need to think about for a few days before he could really know where he stood.

Chapter 7

The following days dragged on for Jason. His mind was filled with Roman and looking for evidence of the hidden paranormal world. When he was out on patrol, he kept an eye out for anything that seemed out of place—the sort of thing he might not have noticed, or have written off as just one of those weird things that happened in San Destino, but now he was searching for the shadow world.

It turned out to be much more obvious than he'd expected. There was strangeness everywhere and he was baffled he'd never seen any of it before. He was looking over the records for Granger Porter, the young man who had come in after the raid and who had been supported by Roman in the station. He didn't have any criminal convictions, had attended the local high school, scored low in his classes, but managed to graduate with his GED. After that, both parents had been killed in a car accident—which may or may not have been a cover for something paranormal, Jason couldn't tell from the file. He had been in and out of homeless shelters, supported living, and the one single room occupancy hotel in San Destino. All of which was to say, while he hadn't been in trouble with the law directly, he had spent a lot of time in the sorts of places where a young person could get themselves mixed up with the wrong sort.

Granger had been released on bail about a day after his arrest when his lawyer finally turned up and argued he was probably in the wrong place at the wrong time and should be let out. It wasn't clear where he was staying now; the house where he had been living previously was still an active crime scene. He was probably a wolf shifter too, given the connection to the Lupin Center. The whole thing rankled at him; Growl wasn't illegal, and arresting everyone in the house and charging them with whatever they could was a misuse of power.

According to the file, Granger had been charged with possession of drug paraphernalia; household items that were innocuous on their own but could also be used to take drugs. Granger had cigarette papers in his room, and a coffee grinder, which could be used to break up the Growl, and roll it into joints as you might with marijuana. To Jason, it was a stretch. The kid had no controlled substances, wasn't known to be a dealer, or a habitual user of any illegal substances, and once he had a criminal conviction, he was much more likely to be picked up again.

Then there was the tip off, or whatever intel had been used to put together the raid. It was hard to understand why someone would dob these people in for smoking an herb that was not illegal and only affected shifters.

Something was sure off about it, but Jason couldn't put his finger on what.

His first instinct was to text Roman and ask his advice, but since their fight the other day, he hadn't contacted him. He would have to re-open the communications channels, he knew, since it was he who said he never wanted to speak to Roman. For his part, Roman was respecting the boundary, something that made him all the more attractive, but also fed that seed of doubt in Jason that he wasn't that into him. Jason shook his head. None of this was helping anything, his shift was over, and he should have clocked out half an hour ago.

*

Friday night at Jack's Bar was their second busiest night of the week. With live music and happy hour drinks from five till six, they usually attracted a solid after-work crew who would then stick around for the band and have some dinner. The menu was more on the fried foods end of the spectrum than Roman thought was healthy, but the patrons didn't buy the healthier options when they tried them, so he had stopped serving them.

It had been nearly a week since Jason had left his place, swearing to never see him again, and it hurt almost as much every time he thought about it, though he admitted he thought of it a little less each day. It had been like torture not to text him good morning, or good night, or when he saw something funny or cute at first, but it was getting easier. Roman couldn't remember who he used to text before Jason; probably no one. Maybe he and the band could work on a new tune or revamp the set-list; that used to be something he filled his time with.

A little after eight that evening, he looked up to see a contingent of people he knew were from the SDPD. They would often have knock off drinks, Thursday and Friday seemed to be their big days, but there were a few every night. He watched them take a booth in the back, and was saddened, but also relieved, to see Jason wasn't with them. He couldn't stare after them for long, people were lining up for drinks and they would get demanding if he stood around mooning over his boyfriend—ex-boyfriend's lack of attendance for too long.

"Can I have a pale ale, please?" The voice was familiar; a warm shiver ran up Roman's spine before he even turned to see Jason standing at the bar.

"Sure, draft okay or do you want a bottle?"

"Draft is fine."

It was impossible for Roman to hide the smile plastered on his face, though he did try to temper it. Jason could just be there for drinks, that's how they'd met after all.

"Here we are." Roman put the tall, frosted glass in front of the gorgeous blond he used to date.

"I, uh… was hoping we could talk. I know the last time we saw each other was left rather tense."

"You could say that."

"I don't want to interrupt while you're working. What time do you knock off?"

"I'm on till eleven."

Jason smiled, and the butterflies in Roman's stomach started trying to escape. He had thought the door was closed on their relationship, it had been days and days, but maybe he'd given up too easily. If there was anything he could do to fix the rift he'd caused between them by hiding and then revealing his true self, he would do it. The time without Jason had taught him there was something more there, and he wanted it back.

"I'll be here." Jason turned and went back to the other cops sitting in the back, as always, part of the group, but still on the outside.

Roman spent the remainder of his shift wishing away the minutes, while stealing glances at Jason across the crowded bar. He was with his colleagues but seemed to mostly be listening to whatever anecdotes they were telling, not telling his own. They weren't his people. Roman wondered who his people really were—certainly the wolf community would welcome him, but he would never understand the experience the way another wolf did. Maybe, if—no, when—they were back on track, he could suggest some hobbies or something to help Jason meet some friends outside of work.

At five past eleven, Roman had taken off his name tag, and signed out on the roster pinned to the back of the storeroom door. Jack's was still pumping, but he was glad to be finished the long shift since he opened that afternoon. When he looked around the bar for Jason; he couldn't see him with the other cops, nor at the bar getting a refill. He briefly checked the men's bathrooms, but he wasn't there either. Roman frowned; had he said he would meet him outside?

Out on the pier, the air was crisp, and the chill of the evening had settled in, though it was still mild as they headed toward the end of summer. He looked around but still saw no sign of Jason. He sniffed the air. Now out of the bar, his wolf-like sense of smell could better pick up Jason's scent in the air; he'd been past a short time ago, back towards the shore.

Roman tried not to think about why he would have been going that way, rather than waiting for him in the bar. He followed his nose past a couple of places that were closed for the night, until he came to an alley where he heard voices.

All the hairs on the back of his neck stood up, and his senses were on high alert—something was wrong, he didn't know what yet, but he wasn't going to be taken unawares. As he moved closer to the voices, he was light on his feet, another of his wolf talents he rarely employed in day-to-day life.

"Why you asking about Growl then, ain't you a cop?" a deep, raspy voice asked. There was something familiar in the voice, but he couldn't place it yet.

"I'm only a rookie, but I know it's not illegal. And I'm not on duty tonight. I was hoping to uh… sample some. I heard you knew how to get some," Jason said.

"I think we should teach the pig a lesson about people who sell recreational substances," another voice said.

"Are you nuts? We can't beat on a cop. That's guaranteed bad news, plus he can identify us."

There was an ominous pause.

"You're right, we gotta kill him."

Roman was shocked by the casual tone the two men had for discussing the cold-blooded murder of a police officer. He could see them now. Two hulking men were standing between Jason and the exit of the alleyway, he was boxed in.

At that moment, Roman knew he had to act, and fast. His best option was to shift into his wolf form and hope the two men weren't shifters too—they weren't wolf shifters, he knew all of the locals. It was likely they were Paranorms of some sort, given their connection to Growl, but Roman was confident he could take them out, or at least buy Jason enough time to get out of the alley and away from danger.

The element of surprise was on his side. The two men didn't know he was there, and it took a few seconds to shift to his wolf self. Once he had shifted, if the men were shifters they would smell him immediately, so he lunged towards them just as the one closer to Jason was raising his hand, a knife gleaming in his fist.

With a snarl, Roman ripped out the throat of the first man, hoping he had time to get to the second, the one holding the knife, before he hurt Jason. The man had turned. He was heavy set, broad shouldered, and bearded. His eyes widened in alarm while he took in the bloodied, lifeless body of his companion.

"I should have known this was a set up, we heard you was hanging out with shifter scum," the man said, his free hand coming up, palm raised, fingers curled as he muttered something under his breath. He must have been a warlock because Roman could feel the shift back to his human shape happening without his control. His vision blurred momentarily as the shift washed over him, and when it cleared, Jason was standing over the body of the warlock, the man's bloody knife in his hand.

"What?" Roman spluttered.

"He was distracted with… whatever he was doing with his hand, and I grabbed the knife and stabbed him in the neck. It seemed like the best course of action available at the time, but uhh…" Jason was trembling. "I think I need to sit down."

Roman stepped forward, taking Jason's wrist and leading him gently to the end of the alley, away from the bodies. "You can put the knife down now."

"Oh." Jason looked at his hand as though remembering he was still holding it.

"I think we should call your colleagues."

"But your face—you've got blood all over you. I can claim self-defense, but what will you do?"

Roman thought for a moment. He knew other wolves who had been forced to take out an enemy in self-defense, and it wasn't an easy path, but the idea of lying or leaving Jason to deal with the fallout on his own was out of the question. "I'll just tell them I bit him. It's not a lie, neither of them are going to contradict me, and well, this is San Destino, stranger things have happened."

Jason laughed, a short hollow sound. "A week ago, I would have said you were exaggerating, but now I know better."

"I'll call for the police; no good asking that lot inside, they're all drunk."

"Let me do it, I'll get a faster response." Jason pulled out his phone. His shaking hands had calmed down a lot since the moment he'd dropped the knife onto the ground. "Yes, this is Officer Jason Bell, San Destino Police, badge number one-nine-seven-seven-five. I need assistance on Providence Pier. Officer involved homicide."

Roman thought that must have been his professional cop voice, it sounded so authoritative, and if the situation had been different, possibly a little bit arousing too. He filed that thought away for later.

"They'll be here shortly. No doubt they'll send everyone on shift, bunch of looky-loos." He gave a half-smile before glancing at his hands again and seeing the blood there.

"What the hell did I walk in on anyway?" Roman took Jason's hand. It would probably compromise evidence, but right then he needed comfort, no doubt Jason did too.

"I heard those two at the bar talking about Growl, and I asked them, innocently I thought, if they knew where a person could get some. They suggested that we go outside where we could hear better and, well, they obviously knew I was police and were willing to kill me for that one question. If they're that violent, maybe that's why we've started raiding for Growl dealers."

"Yeah. Lucky I came to find you."

"You can say that again." Jason squeezed his hand, and Roman heard the distant sound of sirens. "What was that guy doing with his hand?"

"I wouldn't tell your colleagues about that. Best to assume people don't know about the whole paranormal thing, but I think he was a warlock. I'm pretty sure he was forcing me to change back to my human self so he could fight me."

"Right. Warlocks."

The sound of heavy footfalls thundered up the pier towards them.

"Thank you for saving me. Seeing you as the wolf charging towards me, I was equal parts terrified and thankful."

"I know you'll have lots of questions, and I still want to talk about whatever you wanted to talk about, but it looks like the reinforcements are here."

Jason nodded. It was best to stick to human explanations and leave the paranormal world for another time when they were alone.

*

Jason was separated from Roman when the other officers arrived, six in total, only one of whom he had worked with before, the others he knew from seeing them around the station. The sergeant on duty was Hoyt, a burly black man, who he'd been paired with once or twice before. Taller than Jason but not by much, Hoyt was in his late forties, and his dark hair was graying at the temples.

"Now, since this is an officer involved homicide, I have to advise you that you can have your union rep with you when you're questioned. Do you want the rep now?"

Jason thought about it for a moment, then shook his head, deciding he would rather get the preliminaries over with and he could call in the rep later. He wasn't even sure who it was at this point, his mind was somehow both foggy and crystal clear.

"Alright. Tell me in your own words what happened?"

"Uh…" Jason's throat was suddenly parched, and he swallowed before restarting the sentence. "I came out with these two, they had offered to sell me Growl. I believed they didn't know I was on the job, but when we started walking into the alley, I knew I'd made a mistake."

"I see." Hoyt was making notes.

"Anyway, being an idiot, I let myself be boxed into the dead end, the first man," he pointed to the man whose throat he had stabbed only a short time ago, "threatened to hurt me, the other man said they would kill me. The first guy pulled out the knife and came at me. That's when Roman came onto the scene. I'm not really sure what happened but, um, I guess he went for the first guy's throat, and while they were both distracted I got the knife off the first guy and umm, killed him."

"And how did the knife end up there?" Hoyt pointed to where the knife had fallen, halfway back to the entrance of the alley.

"I was, well, shaken by the whole thing. I didn't realize I was still holding it until I was standing there next to that dumpster, and when I noticed, I dropped it. That's when I called nine-one-one."

Hoyt pressed his lips together and noted something. "Were these two guys people you'd encountered before?"

"I don't think so."

"It's a wonder they offered to sell you anything if they didn't know you and hadn't had an introduction from someone they knew. It's not how it's done."

Jason shrugged. "They'd just passed something to someone at the bar and I asked whether I could get some of whatever it was. Having just been on the raid the other day, I recognized the claw marks on the baggie."

Hoyt made a grumbling noise and squeezed the bridge of his nose between thumb and forefinger. "It's all so messy and inconvenient. No doubt there's no CCTV covering this alley. What were you thinking?"

"If I'm being honest, sir, I wasn't thinking. I see how foolish it was for me to go with them without backup. I'm just a rookie and I've got a lot to learn."

"That you do." He glanced over the two bodies, then down at Jason's hands and clothing, both of which were covered in blood. Roman's clothes were also covered, though he'd wiped the blood from his mouth on his sleeve. "You'll have to come down to the station. We'll need your clothes for evidence. I expect we'll be able to get you home after that, but it might take a few hours. Ward will need to speak to you, and you'll have to be cleared before you're allowed back on active duty."

Jason nodded, it all sounded like standard procedure. "What about Roman?"

"He'll need to do the same. I expect neither of you will be charged, but there are no guarantees. Wait here. Don't talk to anyone, I'll be back soon."

Jason folded his hands under his armpits. The night wasn't cold but he was shivering.

It must be the shock, he thought to himself. They hadn't bagged his hands, but they would no doubt want to test the blood under his nails and on his clothes. He wondered if the two men had records, it would be easier to sell the self-defense theory if they had previous violent offences.

*

Processing and taking statements took most of the night, and only after the morning shift had started was Jason allowed out of the cells. He'd been held alone, for his protection, while Roman had been in with two others— he could see him across the corridor but didn't speak to him. He was wearing a white paper jumpsuit as the investigators had taken his clothes.

The officers who had processed and questioned him didn't seem concerned about the incident. It turned out the two deceased were well known to police, though they were new to San Destino. Both had arrests for assaults with weapons, and dealing drugs, though neither had been convicted of more than possession.

"Slippery these two. Seems like they had it coming. I'm sure it'll be fine," Hoyt had said as he opened the cells which smelled of pine disinfectant to put Jason back inside.

The Watch Commander started work at nine and had come down to the cells to speak to him. "Bell," he said with a curt nod. "Come with me, son."

Jason hated when Ward called him son, but it wasn't worth mentioning, just part of the old school bullshit he had to deal with. He followed the older man into his office and took a seat, the paper jumpsuit rustling as he moved.

"I'm sure the others have been over this, but you're on administrative leave pending the outcome of the investigation into the incident last night," Ward said.

"Yes, sir."

"I'll be honest, I didn't think you had that in you. If I'd been a betting man, I would have said we'd be scraping you off the pavement in that alley, but you've proved me wrong."

Jason opened his mouth to reply, but had no idea what to say, and closed it again.

"That's not to say I condone the taking of a life, but by all accounts it's textbook self-defense. We'll have it cleared up in no time." He smiled, a strange sort of response to a subordinate who had just killed a man, but then again, a lot of what happened in the San Destino PD seemed strange to Jason. "I'll have someone take you home. I think Holmes is on shift now if you want her to do it."

"Yes, sir, that would be good."

"Alright. Try not to stress yourself out. We might need you to come back in for some more questions, depending on what the team finds, and I'll be in touch about your roster when you're cleared for duty. You never know, you might even get a medal."

"Uh, thank you, sir."

Ward stood up, as though to indicate the chat was over.

"Is my friend Roman still in holding?"

"I think so. Just a couple of bits of paperwork to be finalized and he can be released as well."

"Would it be alright to stick around until he's ready to go too?"

"That would be fine. I'm sorry we didn't have any other clothes for you," he waved at the jumpsuit, "they're awful uncomfortable those get-ups."

"It's okay, sir. I'll be home soon."

Jason waited in the lobby for about twenty minutes before Riley Holmes strolled out to greet him.

"Roman will be here in a minute, then I'm taking you both home." She looked so good in her uniform, he was always struck by how powerful it made her appear. He didn't think it fit him nearly as well. "You doing okay?"

He nodded, not wanting to say anything at that moment in case he burst into tears or something. Her simple query seemed motherly, and reminded him of the gulf between what he wanted from his own mother, and what he got. She sat beside him, silent, as though understanding it wasn't the time for chat.

Roman walked into the lobby a short time later, also wearing a white paper jumpsuit.

"High fashion for you two, then?" Riley said, standing up to bring Roman over. "I'm taking you home."

"Thanks," Roman mumbled.

They said nothing until they were all in the car. Being in the back of the patrol car was weird, but since he wasn't on duty, he couldn't sit in the front with Riley.

"So, I read the incident report from last night. Tell me what really happened." Riley was regarding them both in the rear-view mirror. Roman looked at him, as though looking for reassurance.

"She knows, we can tell her."

Jason and Roman told Riley the real story of what had happened, including the warlock trick that had forced Roman to shift back.

"Well, I'll be damned."

Jason had already told her that Roman was a shifter, but she didn't mention it, for which he silently thanked her.

"Yeah, if Roman hadn't been there, I would have been toast. Even Ward said he didn't think I had it in me."

"Dick. He never sees anyone's strength unless they're like him." Riley's hands tightened on the steering wheel; she and Ward were frequently on opposing sides of things.

"Do you think they bought the story?"

Riley sighed heavily. "I think they did. Maybe not entirely, but enough to close it as justifiable homicide. Dragging it through the courts, even if it was just Roman, would really be a bad look for the department, so it's in their interests to close it up quickly."

"And if the press gets hold of it?" Roman asked. He'd been quiet most of the ride.

"They'll circle the wagons. It's not police brutality since you weren't on duty, and self-defense with these two is easy for people to understand. They were bad dudes. I can't believe you followed them out of the bar."

"I know. It was stupid, so stupid. If I was in charge, I'd fire me just for that."

Riley chuckled. "No such luck, young one. You'll have to stick around a while longer. The force needs people like you."

"Yeah." Roman squeezed Jason's hand. They pulled up to Jason's place.

"Thanks for the ride, and for listening."

"Any time. I mean that." Riley got out of the car and opened the door for them. "Try to get some rest, and a shower. And don't worry." She waved and drove away.

Jason stood at his front door, Roman a little behind him, his hand hovering in front of the lock. He was fairly sure his roommate was out, but he hadn't had the talk with her about paranormal stuff.

"I don't have to come in, if it's, y'know, awkward," Roman said, his deep rich voice vibrated behind him.

"It's not that." Jason half turned to look at him. "I was trying to figure out if Holly was home, and whether I wanted to do the meeting my roommate thing." He sighed.

"I can go."

"Let me just check the coast is clear. It'll be hectic enough explaining why I didn't come home last night, and why I don't have any clothes without adding wolf shape-shifters and meeting boyfriends to the mix." He tried to smile, but it was such an effort he wasn't sure if it worked.

"Okay, I'll hang here."

Jason opened the door and walked in quietly. The booties on his feet whispered over the hardwood floors. He stuck his head in Holly's room, empty, and she wasn't anywhere else either.

"It's clear," he said as he let Roman into the house. The weight of what had happened the night before felt heavy. Everything had seemed so easy before he knew about all the hidden stuff, but maybe he'd just been ignorant of everything that was happening around him.

"You look like you're going to fall asleep standing up. I would offer to make you coffee but…" He waved his hand in the air. It was the first time Roman had been in his place, and he wouldn't know where anything was.

"I'm sure I can manage to brew a cup before I fall over."

Roman smiled half-heartedly. He looked almost as tired as Jason felt.

They were silent as Jason moved around the kitchen, putting the water on to boil, adding coffee to the French press, waiting as it steeped for a few minutes, then pouring it into two mismatched mugs. He had his with cream and vanilla syrup, a vice he'd developed while attending community college where the coffee was both bitter and tasteless and needed to be masked with something saccharine. Roman had his black.

"Come sit." Jason led the way to the lounge room, to his favorite spot on their big squishy sofa. Roman looked slightly pained, as though unsure where to sit, so Jason patted the cushion next to him. "We need to talk, but maybe you could just sit with me for a bit?"

Roman sat down, and Jason immediately curled into him, their paper jumpsuits crinkling against each other. He smelled of the holding cells, but he also smelled like himself, that deep, musky combination of his soap, cologne, and natural scent. It was comforting, the week they'd been fighting seemed to fade away, and it was just a couple sharing a quiet moment. Jason sipped his coffee. It was pretty good if he did say so himself, although perhaps after the night he'd had his tastebuds weren't to be trusted.

When he was done with his coffee, Roman put his cup onto the coffee table, apparently trying not to disturb their embrace, but failing. "You said we needed to talk."

Jason sighed. "Yeah. I—"

"Let me say something," Roman interrupted. "I was always going to tell you about, y'know, the wolf thing, but part of me was worried you wouldn't want to be with me. Would think I was dangerous. So, I put it to the back of my mind. Then when all that Growl stuff was happening, I knew I needed to tell you sooner than later and … I might have mishandled it." He paused for a moment, running a hand over his face. "I'm sorry for lying to you. I know I had my reasons, but you feeling betrayed is totally understandable, and for that I'm sorry. I hope I can earn your trust back."

"I'm sorry too." Jason took Roman's hands in his, enjoying their reassuring size and weight. "I reacted badly. I know it's not easy to have something about yourself that makes you different, that might make people reject you, hell, I've always been a bit effete and people have been cruel to me… not that being a wolf shifter is the same, but umm, I'm not sure what I'm trying to say but I'm sorry for saying I never wanted to see you again. I missed you the last week."

"I missed you too. I felt like I had been asleep all my life, and now that I knew what real, deep, uh, love could feel like, I didn't want to just go back to existing in the world without it."

"It's a lot to take in, learning the world is different to the way you thought it was your whole life." Jason squeezed his hands. "Wait, did you just say love?"

Roman looked away, his throat flushing red. "I, uh… yeah."

The smile that came across Jason's face felt ready to burst it open. "I know I've had less experience in relationships than you, and we've only known one another for a short time, but I feel the same. I love you, Roman Eldritch."

The goofy lopsided grin on Roman's face set off fireworks in Jason's brain. It might be a bumpy ride getting used to the wolves, and witches and whatever else, but he was confident that with Roman by his side, it would be worth wading through all that.

"I don't know if I've mentioned this, but uh, thanks for saving my life last night."

"No problem. Just…"

"What?" Jason prompted.

"Maybe next time, don't go with drug dealers into alleyways?"

"Absolutely. I promise to never do anything that dumb again." He paused. "Well, I'll do my best, how's that?"

"I'll take that." Roman leaned forward, his eyes lingering on Jason's lips, until they finally met in a kiss that made all their kisses before seem like practice. All the feelings Jason had pushed down when he thought they were over came bubbling up to the surface again and it was hard to keep his hands off Roman. His lover seemed to feel the same, their kisses deepening quickly from tentative to urgent, as they ripped off the jumpsuits and disappeared into Jason's bedroom.

Holly might be out of the house, but he wasn't about to defile the sofa they sat on together, even for the hottest wolf in San Destino.

The End.

About the author

Fleur Blüm, a Melbourne-based writer, performer, and musician, crafts fiction with a romantic twist, infused with feminist themes. Balancing light and dark, she adds humor to narratives exploring tough topics.

Fleur has ten other published novels, and three poetry collections.

You can find out about Fleur, including book links and upcoming releases, at her website: www.fleurblum.com